Spring
Breakup

I can't catch
a break—even
during spring
break...

Praise for

Revenge of the Homecoming Queen

"Debut author Stephanie Hale has written a fabulously quirky and fun tale of homecoming courts, devilish popularity plots, and down-and-out fun . . . Ms. Hale has penned a laugh-out-loud, catty winner . . . Part froufrou couture mixed with amateur sleuthing, this book is one guilty pleasure that you won't mind indulging in."

—TeensReadToo.com

"Meg Cabot better watch her back because Stephanie Hale is giving her a run for her money." —*Book Divas*

"They didn't write teen books like this when I was in high school—and it's a darned shame . . . Snappy dialogue + good characterization + fun story = a terrific teen read!"

—*Fresh Fiction*

"Her narration is strong—confident and ridiculous-in-a-good-way amusing . . . with some of the secondary characters getting laugh-out-loud funny one-liners." —*The Ya Ya Yas*

"*Revenge of the Homecoming Queen* is an awesome book. I loved how Stephanie Hale jumps from one conflict to the next. It kept me hanging on throughout the story." —*Flamingnet*

"Debut author Stephanie Hale sets up her Aspen series in a winning way. Can't wait to read what happens to Aspen next." —*Enchanting Reviews*

"The plot moves quickly, and lots of twists keep the reader going." —*Romantic Times*

Berkley JAM titles by Stephanie Hale

REVENGE OF THE HOMECOMING QUEEN
TWISTED SISTERS
SPRING BREAKUP

Spring Breakup

Stephanie Hale

BERKLEY JAM, NEW YORK

THE BERKLEY PUBLISHING GROUP
Published by the Penguin Group
Penguin Group (USA) Inc.
375 Hudson Street, New York, New York 10014, USA
Penguin Group (Canada), 90 Eglinton Avenue East, Suite 700, Toronto, Ontario M4P 2Y3, Canada
(a division of Pearson Penguin Canada Inc.)
Penguin Books Ltd., 80 Strand, London WC2R 0RL, England
Penguin Group Ireland, 25 St. Stephen's Green, Dublin 2, Ireland (a division of Penguin Books Ltd.)
Penguin Group (Australia), 250 Camberwell Road, Camberwell, Victoria 3124, Australia
(a division of Pearson Australia Group Pty. Ltd.)
Penguin Books India Pvt. Ltd., 11 Community Centre, Panchsheel Park, New Delhi—110 017, India
Penguin Group (NZ), 67 Apollo Drive, Rosedale, North Shore 0632, New Zealand
(a division of Pearson New Zealand Ltd.)
Penguin Books (South Africa) (Pty.) Ltd., 24 Sturdee Avenue, Rosebank, Johannesburg 2196,
South Africa

Penguin Books Ltd., Registered Offices: 80 Strand, London WC2R 0RL, England

This book is an original publication of The Berkley Publishing Group.

This is a work of fiction. Names, characters, places, and incidents either are the product of the author's imagination or are used fictitiously, and any resemblance to actual persons, living or dead, business establishments, events, or locales is entirely coincidental. The publisher does not have any control over and does not assume any responsibility for author or third-party websites or their content.

PRINTING HISTORY
Berkley JAM trade paperback edition / March 2009

Library of Congress Cataloging-in-Publication Data

Hale, Stephanie.
 Spring breakup / Stephanie Hale. — Berkley trade paperback ed.
   p. cm.
   Summary: In Las Vegas for spring break with friends Rand, Angel, and Lucas, nineteen-year-old sorority girl Aspen investigates the disappearance of a beauty contestant by taking her place as Illinois's representative in the Miss Teen Queen pageant.
   ISBN 978-0-425-22592-9 (Berkley trade pbk.)   [1. Beauty contests—Fiction.   2. Missing persons—Fiction.   3. Dating (Social customs)—Fiction.   4. Las Vegas (Nev.)—Fiction.
5. Mystery and detective stories.]   I. Title.

PZ7.H138244Spr 2009
[Fic]—dc22   2008048606

PRINTED IN THE UNITED STATES OF AMERICA

10   9   8   7   6   5   4   3   2   1

For the three guys I'll never break up with.

Acknowledgments

Thank you to Cindy Hwang and Leis Pederson for allowing Aspen and her friends into the Berkley family. I will be eternally grateful.

Hugs go out to Jenny Bent for everything you have done for me. You're the bomb!

More hugs to Tina Ferraro and Tera Lynn Childs for being my writing bffs. Thank you both for always being there when I need to vent or be neurotic.

For my three guys, thank you for giving me a happier life than I could have ever dreamed. I love you all!

One

"What do you mean you lost my suitcase?" I ask, hoping that I misunderstood the clerk at the baggage claim desk. Maybe English isn't her first language. That has to be it because there is no way my spring break is starting off like this.

"We didn't lose your bag, Ms. Brooks. We just can't find it," she says, grinning like some deranged robot. I think the severe bun she has going on is cutting off her oxygen supply because she is completely oblivious to the gravity of this situation. I can feel my face going up in flames, which is never good, because red isn't even close to my best color. "Our airline has a ninety-seven percent customer satisfaction score for finding lost luggage," she boasts.

"Yet my purple suitcase that is covered in sparkles

remains in the other three percent," I shout. I know I shouldn't be pitching such a fit, but how can I be rational when my entire wardrobe is probably being auctioned off on eBay by a disgruntled Vegas Now employee right this very moment? I'm not just being paranoid. I saw the look that stewardess gave me when I complained about the mini Coke and the nitrate-filled sandwich she gave me. Can I help it that I was worried about getting low blood sugar?

"You don't have to take that tone with me," the clerk says, giving me elevator eyes. She pauses on the sleeve of my cashmere cardigan. I follow her eyes to the stain that is still permeating my nostrils with noxious fumes. Just as I am about to demand to speak to her superior, I feel a comforting pressure against the middle of my back. I glance over to see Rand, my perfect boyfriend of nearly one year. I can feel my anger melting away as he moves behind me and rests his chin on top of my head. I don't even care that he is totally messing up my hair. With Rand pressing against me, I don't even remember what I was mad about. Rand could tell me that olive green is the new black and I wouldn't even care. That's how much I love him.

"No offense, but I think you are past your expiration date," the clerk says, fanning her hand in front of her face. I can't help but laugh, even though part of me wants to counter with "Oh, yeah? Well I don't think shoulder pads made a comeback." But I suppose it isn't her fault that the airline makes her wear such a dorky-looking uniform.

"Do you see why I'm so upset about losing my bag?" I plead, gesturing toward the stain.

"There's nothing more I can do. Leave a contact phone number and we'll get in touch with you if—I mean, *when*—your bag arrives," she says smugly.

I start to reach over the counter to pull her bun a little tighter but Rand intercepts the gesture smoothly.

"Here's my cell phone number and we really appreciate all your help, Marcia," Rand says, getting her name off the tag on her sweater. He hands her a scrap of paper with his digits scrawled on it, then holds his hand out to shake hers. I know his whole catch-more-flies-with-honey theory has its merits, but after the day I've had, I would much rather put a smack-down on Marcia than thank her. She winks at Rand and I have to fight the urge to throw up in my mouth.

I secure my Dooney on my shoulder, thank God it wasn't an airline casualty—not that I'd check it in a million years—and walk away. Rand guides me over to our traveling companions, Lucas and Angel, who are practically making out on top of their suitcases.

"It figures. Lucas gets his suitcase full of muscle tees and cargo shorts but my suitcase full of Mom's new designs is AWOL," I say, disgusted. Lucas shrugs as if this is going to bring me some comfort. I stomp my kitten heel–clad foot on the airport floor and wonder how the world can be so cruel sometimes.

"I'm really sorry I threw up on you," Angel offers, making Lucas cringe as he just realizes Angel hasn't brushed her teeth since the unpleasant plane sickness incident.

"It's okay. You warned me. I just thought you were joking when you asked me to pass you the puke bag." I let out a sigh of defeat as Rand starts kneading my shoulders. I can't catch a break, even on spring break.

This is so not how I pictured my first spring break. I knew Las Vegas was a bad idea. I mean, what is there to do here for nineteen-year-olds anyway? It's not like we can gamble. And what about the golden tan and sand between my perfectly pedicured toes I had imagined? R & R— Rand and rays. That's all I wanted.

"Everything is going to be fine, Aspen. They'll find your bag, but in the meantime, this means we need to go shopping," Rand says, always knowing the right thing to say to perk me up.

"You're right. Vegas is supposed to have some decent couture. I guess this doesn't have to be a complete tragedy." I smile. I stand on my tippy toes and give Rand a peck on the lips. I always thought that guys quit growing by now but Rand just keeps getting taller. It's kind of romantic having to look up to gaze into his eyes. The guys pick up the suitcases that survived the trip and we move outside to load onto a shuttle to our hotel. The temperature is at least thirty degrees warmer than when we left Illinois, so

I strip down to my cardigan shell and stuff my tainted cardigan in my Dooney. I feel better already.

I hear something fluttering above me. I look up, surprised to see palm trees. Palm trees in Las Vegas? I only expected to see cactus. Maybe there's hope for this place yet. I soak in the warm breeze while Lucas and Rand load the suitcases. Angel seems to sense that I need a minute to acclimate myself so she stands next to me, silent, but bobbing up and down on her heels with excitement. I guess after living with me for almost a full year now at the Beta sorority house she is getting pretty good at gauging my mood.

Who would have ever thought that my onetime high school nemesis would turn out to be one of my best friends? I can hardly wait until our five-year class reunion to go back and shock the crap out of some people. It turns out that Angel and I aren't so different after all. She pretty much saved my life last year after my psycho ex-sorority sisters, the Zetas, turned out to be a whole lot more evil than their cotton candy–pink sweatshirts would have you think. She went behind my back and called Detective Harry Malone, who attempted to save the day. Too bad for him that I already had it under control. Well, kind of. Of course, I was the one who figured out the mystery of his niece Mitzi's disappearance. Unfortunately it wasn't some Ted Bundy knockoff but my very own roommate, Charm.

She was right under my perfectly powdered nose the whole time but I never suspected her until it was almost too late. In my defense, I was a bit busy trying to ward off the advances of Rand's ultra-rich, uber-slimy roommate, Koop. And keeping Rand off the sauce proved to be a bit of a challenge, too. Don't even get me started on how hard my midterms were. After all that, is it so wrong to expect a little break?

A few minutes later, we are zipping down the Strip.

"Look, Aspen," Rand says, gripping my shoulders and turning me toward the huge back window of the shuttle. I'm so tired that I don't even remember getting on. The long day of travel, lost luggage, and being mistaken for an airsickness bag are starting to kick in. I wonder if our hotel has a spa? I so need to be pampered.

When I look up, I can't believe my eyes. The Strip is like a giant display of Christmas lights that lasts all year long. I try to take in every sight as we whiz through the middle of town. The lights and air are invigorating. Rand slips his left hand in my right and our fingers intertwine perfectly. He flashes me one of his dazzling smiles and my stomach drops. Suddenly I realize it doesn't matter where we are, as long as Rand and I are together. Seven fun-filled, drama-less days with my perfect boyfriend. Even without luggage, this is still a dream come true.

◎

"Why won't you just tell us where we are staying?" I plead with Angel.

She mimes zipping her mouth shut and throwing away an imaginary key. As if an imaginary lock could keep that trap shut! Against my better judgment, I left all the travel arrangements up to Angel. She swore that she knew some awesome discount website where we could get suites at one of the finest hotels in Vegas for next to nothing. I'm dying to know which hotel we are spending the next seven days at. Our shuttle zips past the Planet Hollywood Resort & Casino, the Paris, and Caesars Palace. I'm almost positive that our destination is the Venetian. I practically get shivers imagining how romantic a gondola ride with Rand will be.

"You look happy," Rand whispers into my ear.

"How could I be anything else? I'm here with you in the most exciting city on the planet. What more could a girl ask for? Well, besides her luggage?" I smile, sinking into his chest and nuzzling his neck. Rand has the best smell ever. Not his cologne, although that's yummy too, but his personal scent. I can't get enough of it.

"We've got a room for that." Angel nudges me playfully. "Let's get you guys to it."

We all pile out of the shuttle, anxious to get a look at our new digs for the next seven days. I'm in shock that at almost midnight tourists still crowd the sidewalk. I glance around looking for the canals I've only ever seen on the hotel website. I finally spot a giant cove but to my dismay it is inhabited by a giant pirate ship with billowing fire engine–red sails. I glance up to the hotel behind it to see PIRATE'S COVE in flashing neon letters.

"Why are we at Pirate's Cove?" I demand.

"This is where we are staying. Isn't it divine?" Angel beams. Lucas ogles a few scantily clad girls walking a planklike walkway and nods his head in agreement.

"I've heard good things about this place," Rand offers, knowing I'm disappointed.

"I thought we were staying at the Venetian," I say, pouting.

I really don't mean to be so hard to get along with, but today has been excruciating. I've been puked on, had my mom's original designs lost, and have only had half a can of Coke and a sandwich made with unidentified meat products as sustenance. But none of that is Angel's fault (except the puke), and when I see her face fall, I realize I'm acting like a big baby.

"This place is awesome, Angel. I can't believe you got us reservations here. I can't wait to see our rooms." I beam with false excitement. Rand squeezes my arm, which is his nonverbal way of saying that he is proud of me for being a big enough person not to throw a tantrum about staying at a lame, pirate-themed hotel.

"Arrrr . . ." Lucas growls in his best pirate voice. I roll my eyes at Rand, who covers a laugh with a fake cough. The other three grab their bags while I hold the lobby door open for them. The slightest scent of a Ben & Jerry's waffle cone hits my nostrils, and I grin, thinking this might not be such a bad place to hang my Dooney for a week after all.

My grin is replaced by a look of confusion very quickly. I glance around at the wall-to-wall bodies crowding the lobby. A giant banner hanging across the lobby quickly explains why: WELCOME TO THE MISS TEEN QUEEN PAGEANT. Our tiny posse is swallowed up by gaggles of girls with fake tans, reconstructed smiles, and more plastic than Barbie.

"Meet me at the reception desk," Rand yells to me as I find myself against the crowd, struggling, like a salmon trying to swim upstream, but losing out to their buoyant chests. When I finally break free I'm in the casino surrounded by hundreds of slot machines. I've never understood how people could get addicted to gambling. I mean, why sink hundreds of dollars into a stupid machine when you can go buy a new Dooney? But the hypnotic lights and the sound of money clinking has me reaching into my pocket for a quarter.

"Don't even think about it," a buff security guard says to me, just as I go to drop the coin into the slot.

"What?" I ask, playing coy.

"You don't look a day over seventeen," he responds, trying his best to look mean.

"Uh, excuse me. I'm nineteen," I retort, then slap my hand over my mouth as I realize I just totally busted myself out.

"You'd better run along and get yourself some beauty sleep. The competition is pretty fierce," he says, smiling as a leggy blonde in Daisy Dukes and high heels saunters by.

"Eww . . . I'm so not here for the pageant." There was a time in my life when I used to beg my parents to let me burst onto the pageant circuit. Then my mom watched some documentary about pageant moms and said she'd let me join a cult first. After that, it kind of lost its luster.

"Yeah, now that you mention it, you seem a little too smart to be here for the pageant." He laughs. A part of me wants to stick up for the pageant girls. Sure, there's a Miss South Carolina 2007 in every bunch, but most of the girls are here to win scholarship money and prizes, but I don't really want to get myself into trouble before I even check in. I flash him a smile, then start to battle my way back into the main lobby toward the reception desk. I'm so happy that I decided to bring my Dooney tote as a carry-on because it helps me shove my way through the contestants and reunite with Rand.

I'm making pretty good headway until I get bum-rushed by a girl with a rack that rivals Pam Anderson's.

"Oops. My bad." She giggles. I growl at her then rush into a hotel alcove before I can be accosted by any more silicone.

"There is no way I'm dropping out now. No matter how bad I want to," I hear a voice say from behind me. I turn to see a girl standing with her back to me talking into a cell phone. I can't see her face but she definitely isn't dressed like a pageant contestant in her cutoff jean shorts and T-shirt.

"My parents need this money, and nothing is going to stop me from getting it for them," she says desperately.

I feel guilty for eavesdropping but I can't help thinking how cool it is that this girl is doing something she doesn't want to just to help out her parents. It reminds me of how much I helped my mom get back on track after discovering her shopping addiction.

I wonder what she's doing that she doesn't want to do? Wet T-shirt contest at The Palms? Passing out porn on the Strip? Maybe she's planning to rob the casino! Or maybe I've just watched *Ocean's Eleven* too many times.

I'm not taking any chances. I slip out of the alcove before I overhear enough to make me an accomplice. I duck and weave my way through hair extensions and spray tans until I spot Rand.

"I was getting worried. I was afraid they had kidnapped you and injected you with silicone." He laughs.

"Lucas, stop gawking," Angel yells while jamming her credit card back into her wallet.

"Sorry, babe, but I'd have to be dead not to notice all these wenches," Lucas defends himself.

"Lucas has decided to talk like a pirate the entire week," Rand informs me, holding a finger gun to his temple.

"Okay, here we go," Angel says, handing me a key card. "You guys are on the twentieth floor and we are on the thirty-second."

"Wait, what? We don't even have adjoining rooms?" I ask.

"Like I really want to hear you and Rand getting it on all night?" Angel says, sticking her finger down her throat.

"Don't even get me started on who has more experience, Angel," I warn her. "Besides, I promised my parents that Rand and I wouldn't be sharing a room."

"You cannot be serious," Angel says, flipping her ebony hair over her shoulder.

Okay, I didn't exactly lie to Angel. I mean, my parents are under the assumption that I'm bunking with Angel, and as much as I love falling asleep in Rand's arms, it just feels kind of slutty to be sharing a hotel room together. I mean, we aren't exactly virgins, but I just think some things should be a mystery.

"I am very serious." I stare her down and she finally relents and hands Rand her key card.

"God, Aspen. Thanks for the blue balls," Lucas spouts, jamming the elevator UP button.

"Lucas, please do not talk to milady like that," Rand jokes. I know deep down Rand would probably rather share a room with me than Lucas but I'm just not going to force myself to do something I'm not comfortable with. That's just the kind of girl I am.

"Why don't we all go get unpacked and then meet back down here in a half hour to grab a bite?" Rand suggests. Lucas and Angel, still in full pouting mode, nod their heads briefly in agreement. Suddenly I wonder if

I might need a vacation from my vacation after spending 24/7 with this duo. Rand and I lock eyes and I realize he is thinking the exact same thing.

⊚

"I bought you something," Rand says, pitching something black toward my chest. I catch the soft object, a T-shirt, and unwad it.

"Oh, that's hilarious," I say sarcastically. I put the T-shirt up to my chest so that Lucas and Angel can see it. It has a picture of a treasure chest overflowing with gems that reads, "Give up the booty." Classic Rand.

"You needed something to sleep in." Rand laughs. I give him a wink and shove the offending T-shirt into my purse.

"Why don't you swabs grab some grub while I hit the head?" Lucas says, pointing toward a restaurant in the lobby. He cracks himself up and takes off in the other direction for the bathroom.

"You are so going to thank me for not having to share a room with him," I tell Angel. She smiles and nods and leads us toward the restaurant. The pageant mob seems to have cleared out a bit, with just a few freshly glossed contestants remaining. Maybe this pageant won't interfere with our vacation after all.

A frazzled waitress leads us to a booth sandwiched in between two groups of girls. Each booth holds two contestants (I know this because they are wearing their obnoxious sashes with their state name on them) and two older women, probably pageant moms or chaperones. The contestants visually size up Angel and me.

"We're just on spring break," I announce, trying to save them the trouble of sharpening their claws.

"Oh, that's nice. Where are you all from?" one of the contestants asks. I can't read her sash from where I'm standing, but I'd put money on her being a Midwestern girl. She is naturally pretty and stands out against the back-drop of fake blondes and cosmetic surgery addicts I've seen so far. I would put money on her to win in a heart-beat. You know, *if* I was a gambling kind of girl. Then I recognize her as the badly dressed potential casino robber from the alcove. Or not. I guess she was talking about be-ing in the pageant and not pulling off a casino heist. I can't help but be a little disappointed that she isn't the ring-leader of some female bank robber team.

"We're from Illinois," Angel answers, then goes back to reading her menu.

"Oh my gosh, that's where I'm from. Derrytown, born and bred," she exclaims in an octave so high I'm positive my water glass might shatter.

"We're from Comfort," I reply, knowing this conver-sation isn't going to end anytime soon.

"Jeez, we're practically neighbors. Hey, do you guys know L—" she starts to ask, then breaks off and jumps across the booth like a maniac. She is a blur of cutoff jean shorts and a pink John Deere T-shirt with matching Chuck Taylors. Not exactly pageant couture but at least she coordinated her T-shirt and shoes. I don't realize what she is doing until she tackles an unsuspecting Lucas, who is approaching our table. She jumps right into his arms and he manages to catch her.

"What the . . ." Angel bolts out of our booth and heads toward them with fire shooting from her eyes.

"Mmm . . . dinner and a show." I laugh, hardly able to believe that even a thousand miles away Lucas has some girl baggage.

"All I wanted was a cheeseburger," Rand says, defeated.

"Why are you touching my boyfriend?" Angel asks calmly. She grabs her hair and wraps the elastic band from her wrist around it forming a ponytail, preparing for battle.

"Should we do something?" Rand asks nervously.

"Everything will be okay unless she takes off her shoes. If she does that just run for the door," I tell him. Angel's jealousy is relentless. She always thinks every girl alive wants a piece of Lucas. I'd love to set her straight, but considering Lucas is my ex-boyfriend, I don't think she would believe me.

"Angel, calm down. This is Emerson Chambers. We were in 4-H together for a million years," Lucas explains, lowering Emerson back to the ground.

"She's your girlfriend? Oh my gosh, I'm so glad you

aren't in the pageant or I'd never have a chance," Emerson tells Angel. Flattery will get you everywhere with Angel Ives.

"Oh, thanks. It's nice to meet you, Emerson," Angel says, fighting to hide her fangs. Lucas wraps his muscular arms around Angel and she becomes almost human again.

"This is so crazy that you're here. So you're doing this pageant thing?" Lucas asks, leading Angel back to our booth.

"You know me, I'm more comfortable in overalls, but I thought I'd try the girly-girl thing, just this once," Emerson says, rolling her eyes. She's one of those girls who has absolutely no concept of her outside beauty, which just makes her that much more beautiful. I hate girls like that. But she gets major snaps for competing in the pageant just to try to win the prize money for her parents. I have a feeling Emerson would rather be off throwing cow patties than strutting her stuff on a runway.

"Hi, Mrs. Chambers," Lucas says to a heavily made-up woman who is scooting over to let Emerson back into the booth. I take a long look at the pleasant woman and wonder if she realizes that her daughter is only parading around in a sash for her. Probably not. She's probably been praying for her tomboy daughter to wear a dress for years.

"Hello, Lucas. You aren't here to elope, are you?" she asks jokingly.

"God, no. Just grabbing a little quality time with my wench." Lucas laughs, shoving Angel into the booth. She kicks him once she slides in and he grimaces while waving good-bye to Emerson.

"How is it humanly possible that we travel all the way to Las Vegas and run into one of your exes?" Angel spouts.

"I told you. She's an old 4-H buddy. We didn't get it on. We just built a bookshelf together. Get over it," Lucas says angrily, then yanks his menu in front of his face.

"Ah, young love," I tease them, laying my head on Rand's shoulder. I'm so exhausted right now that food doesn't even sound good. I close my eyes and almost drift away thinking about spending the day at the pool tomorrow, and then I remember the dam trip, and stifle a moan. We promised Rand a trip to Hoover Dam and, unfortunately, he hasn't forgotten.

"What do you mean it's been denied?" a voice says nervously from behind me. "Try it again."

"I tried it five times, ma'am. I'm sorry, but you'll have to call your credit card company," another female voice says.

"Mom, don't you have any cash?" asks a voice that I recognize as Emerson's.

"It's all in my other purse upstairs," the first voice—that I now recognize as belonging to Mrs. Chambers—answers back nervously. I sit up and whisper across the table to Lucas.

"I think your friend needs some cash," I say, gesturing behind me. Lucas gets up and walks back to Emerson's booth. Emerson explains that her mother left her money upstairs in her other purse and Lucas offers to help them out. They reluctantly take the money then hurriedly scoot out of their booth.

"It was really nice to meet you all, especially you, Angel," Emerson says, giving a little wave. Angel flashes her a venomous smile.

Lucas slides back into the booth and picks up his menu.

"I can't believe you gave her money," Angel says disgustedly.

"They are good people, Angel. Her parents' dairy farm isn't doing so great these days. I can't believe they can even afford to be here," Lucas says sadly.

"She must not be doing so bad if she's buying evening gowns for pageants," Angel smarts off. "Or maybe she's got herself a sugar daddy."

"She's probably here for the prize money, Angel," I say, trying to shut her up. I love Angel but sometimes her insecurity about Lucas drives me insane. If he hasn't left her yet, he probably isn't going to; I wish she could just realize that.

The same frazzled waitress who sat us rushes up to take our order.

"I'm not even hungry anymore," Angel says, jumping

over Lucas to get out of the booth. Lucas contemplates the menu for a second, sighs, then takes off after Angel.

"Nothing for me," I tell the waitress, who turns and walks to another booth.

"All I wanted was a cheeseburger . . ." Rand trails off.

Two

It took some time but I finally convinced Angel that the entire female species does not consider Lucas Riley the Sexiest Man Alive. They made up—actually, they are still making up—under a palm tree beside the Strip.

"It's two A.M. Actually, it's four A.M., Illinois time. I'm tired and starving. Can we please just get something to eat and go to bed? Our Hoover Dam tour leaves in eight hours and I don't want everybody so exhausted that they don't even enjoy it," Rand whines uncharacteristically. I don't have the heart to tell him that sleep or no sleep he is the only one excited about going to see a giant hole in the desert.

"Lucas, Angel, are you guys coming to get something to eat or not?" I yell, even though I'm not sure even being doused with ice-cold water would get their attention.

"Fine, we're out of here." Rand and I turn to leave and just like I suspected our travel companions trot up behind us giggling and grabbing each other's butt.

"Look, there's an all-you-can-eat buffet right there," Rand says, pointing to a strip mall. A buffet in a strip mall? Every fiber of my body tells me that it is so wrong to eat at a place announcing loose penny slots, but one glance at Rand and I nod and follow him in.

"How many you got?" some dude says in a fake mobsterlike voice.

"Four," Rand answers, pulling his wallet out. Lucas, being the cheapskate he is, doesn't attempt to move for his.

"Ten bucks," the man says, holding his hand out. Rand pays him and he hands us a ticket and points to the back of the room where a buffet cart stands.

"I'll get you next time, matie," Lucas says, draping his arm around Angel and leading the way to the buffet. Rand catches my eye and winks; his way of telling me he won't ever see that money. As much as I hate it when Lucas takes advantage of Rand's generosity, I guess being out five bucks for dinner isn't such a big deal. I can hardly wait to see the buffet that costs two dollars and fifty cents a person.

As we approach the food cart I am very disturbed that no sneeze guards are present. The only thing that keeps me from running out is the fact that we are the only ones here and the food looks amazing. There is fried chicken, pizza, baked potatoes, macaroni and cheese, and my personal favorite, crab legs. I grab a plate and start piling it high with crab legs. I find a small bowl and fill it with drawn butter. I'm practically drooling just thinking about the first bite of tender crabmeat dipped in the warm butter.

"That's my girl," Rand says, as I scoot into a nearby booth and begin chowing down before any of them are even sitting.

Everyone is famished and we spend the meal mostly in silence with the exception of a few grunts of pleasure. It is a comfortable silence, one that comes from being with people who know each other well enough that they don't have to force small talk.

It is almost incomprehensible to think that just two short years ago, Angel was my nemesis, Lucas was my boyfriend (I know, right?), and I didn't even know that Rand Bachrach existed.

I glance over at Rand, who is licking chicken grease off his fingers. How could such an amazing guy have flown under my radar for so long? Rand catches me spying on him and gives me a wink. A slot machine starts chiming and even though I'm not the winner, I still feel like the luckiest girl alive to be here with Rand.

Eventually we leave the restaurant and take a short walk down the Strip. I need some exercise after practically eating my body weight in crab.

"It really is beautiful here," Angel says, gazing up at the lights of the billion-dollar hotels. We all agree but are too tired to say anything. Suddenly a shady-looking guy appears from out of nowhere and hands something to Lucas and Rand. I'm startled at first, thinking maybe we are going to get robbed. But when I see the pamphlet full of half-naked women I realize it's nothing to worry about.

"Wait a minute. You come back here," Angel screams to his retreating figure. "This crap ruins families. You should be ashamed of yourself. Why don't you get a real job?" Angel continues screaming, throwing the pamphlet into the street. The man doesn't even turn around. She bursts into tears and Lucas pulls her close.

Our peaceful stroll down the Strip is cut drastically short by pornography. Not just any pornography but the same smut that ruined her family and had a brief stint in my locker when Angel decided to redecorate for me. Angel's dad used to travel here for business and her mom found suitcases full of porn that he was dragging home. It was the beginning of the end for Mr. and Mrs. Ives. Angel still has days when she can barely comprehend that she will have to choose who to spend the next holiday with. Broken families suck. I'm glad my parental unit is still fully intact.

Rand puts his arm around me and squeezes me tight. We wait quietly until Lucas calms Angel down, then we head back to Pirate's Cove.

On our way back we pass by the buffet again. This time I notice neon bells lighting up the window and realize that the buffet doubles as a wedding chapel.

"Check it out, you guys," I say, pointing and laughing.

"Not only can you get all-you-can-eat crab legs but you can get hitched, too."

"Let's do it," Angel says, pulling Lucas toward the storefront.

I decide to join in the fun and start dragging Rand, while humming the bridal march.

"Very funny, Angel," Lucas says, shaking her off. Rand and I are still laughing, wondering if Elvis will be our witness, when we realize that the mood has taken a serious turn.

"So I'm good enough for now, but not forever," Angel says, tears rolling down her cheeks.

"What the hell, Angel? We're only nineteen years old. Gimme a break," Lucas pleads.

"You don't even love me," Angel cries out, then bolts across the street to our hotel.

Angel doesn't really want to get married. This is just more residual crap left over from her parents' divorce. She's constantly testing Lucas to see how much he loves her.

"And I thought I was high maintenance. You two put me to shame," I say, leaning over to peck Rand on the lips. "I'll handle this. We'll see you in the morning." I wave good-bye and take off after Angel.

☺

"If you keep acting like a psycho, Lucas is going to dump you," I tell Angel, not bothering to sugarcoat it. I am sprawled out on my queen-size bed wearing the T-shirt Rand gave me. I am so ready to get some shut-eye and I really hope to talk some sense into Angel quickly.

"You're right, as usual, Aspen. I don't know what I was thinking," she replies, not glancing up from the giant phonebook she is paging through. Every so often I see her mark a page with a black Sharpie.

That was easy. Too easy. Angel Ives never backs down without a fight. That's why she used to be such a formidable opponent in the halls of our high school. But tonight, or should I say, this morning, I'm just too tired to deal with her. I scoot under my sheets and drift away, trying not to think about how in a few hours I'll be crammed onto a tour bus on my way to see a giant concrete hole in the ground. But considering it's the only thing that Rand asked to do on this trip, I guess I can make the sacrifice. I can't wait to spend the rest of our vacation basking in the sun drinking mocktinis.

@

The first thing I see when I wake up are the red numbers glaring at me from my bedside table. 6:13. Why in the world am I awake so early? Then my stomach clenches, I throw back the sheets and run to the bathroom.

As for what happens next, let's just say that I'm pretty sure I just backed into a smaller size, and not by choice.

"What's going on in here?" Angel says, pushing the door open. "Oh, gross, Aspen. It really stinks in here."

"Gee, I'm so sorry that me dying caused a stench," I squeak out, my head lying on the cool ceramic tile. I don't even care if all those *20/20* stories about maids not really cleaning hotel rooms properly are true right now.

"I can't handle this," she says, closing the door. So much for being my new bff. Not that anybody could ever replace Tobi—who I begged to come on break with us but she and her girlfriend Pippi went to Cabo instead—but Angel was running a close second, until now.

I heave into the toilet again and swear for a second that I can hear Ariel, from *The Little Mermaid*, giggling evilly. Great. Now I'm delirious.

I grab a hand towel and lay it beneath my head, not having enough energy to keep moving from the toilet to the floor. A few seconds later, I feel someone holding my hair back and wiping my face with a cool washcloth. I guess Angel knew what was good for her and came back to be my nursemaid after all.

"You're going to be all right," I hear Rand's soothing voice tell me. Okay, so Angel still kind of sucks for shirking her bff responsibilities, but at least she called Rand.

"No more crab, ever," I say weakly.

"It's okay, don't talk," Rand says, continuing to wipe my forehead.

What says *I love you* more than holding your girl-friend's hair out of the toilet? I am such a lucky girl.

⌒

"It wasn't your crab. I didn't eat Sebastian," I yell out, waking myself up. I bolt up in bed then immediately fall back into my pillow. I was having a horrible nightmare that the Little Mermaid was chasing me with King Triton's trident, trying to spear me because she thought I ate her crab friend. "I feel like crap," I whine, holding my shrunken stomach.

"Dude, I've never seen somebody throw up that much," Lucas says, spinning around in a chair next to the desk in our room.

"Lucas, give her a break. She's really sick," Rand says, giving him a glare that means business.

"Way to ruin our vacation, Aspen," Angel says.

Weakly, I flip her my middle finger. Rand is sitting beside me in bed, stroking my hair. I swear Rand's hair rubs could cure cancer. I feel a little better already.

"What time is it? Did we miss the tour?" I ask, worried. All of the other tours are booked and I know how bad Rand wants to go.

"It's okay, Aspen. I'll see the Hoover Dam another time," Rand says, trying to hide his disappointment.

"We could still go. The bus hasn't left yet," Angel

offers, hiking her jean skirt up to straddle Lucas on the chair. They twirl around together, kissing, and I feel my stomach start to churn again. I'm thinking the dramatic duo is back together.

"You have to go," I tell Rand, even though I really just want him to stay with me.

"I'm not leaving you. You might have salmonella, or food poisoning, or the Norwalk virus, or something worse."

"I feel better already. I think I got it all out of my system and I'm fine now," I lie. Rand sacrifices so much for me and there is no way I'm going to deny him this tour.

"At least she doesn't look green anymore," Angel adds, swaying back and forth, making me dizzy.

"I don't want you to miss this, Rand. I'll be fine. I'm sure the hotel has a doctor. I'll have him take a look at me then I'll order some chicken soup from room service," I say, weak from talking so much but trying not to let it show.

"It's no big deal," Rand says, looking all around the hotel room, refusing to make eye contact with me.

"Whatever, Rand. It's all you've talked about for the last two weeks. Aspen can put on her big-girl panties and take care of herself," Angel says. She smiles and winks at me, knowing she could never get away with talking to me like that if I were in fighting condition.

"Speaking of panties, did the airline ever call?" I ask,

suddenly realizing how gross I feel and wanting to take a shower and change clothes. Rand shakes his head and I groan. "I guess I'll be borrowing your big-girl panties, Angel." She makes a disgusted face.

"I could go buy you something," Rand offers sweetly.

"That's okay," I answer, a little too quickly, and Angel snickers. But after the T-shirt, I'm scared to see what an entire outfit that Rand would pick out would look like.

"You could just lie around in your birthday suit," Lucas offers, getting a playful slap from Angel.

"What are you wearing?" I ask, focusing clearly on Lucas for the first time. He has a black eye patch with a white skull and crossbones over one eye, a matching black T-shirt, camo cargo shorts, and what looks to be a plastic sword hanging from his side.

"Arrr . . ." he says, grabbing the sword and holding it to Angel's neck. She swoons, then acts like she faints in his arms. He replaces the sword on his side and laughs.

"Wake up, wench. You know I'd never really kill ya, not with the way you can shiver me timbers." They both practically die laughing and I'm positive I'm going to hurl again.

"Please take them and go," I beg Rand. If I have to listen to Lucas's pirate talk all day, I know I will try slitting my own throat with his plastic sword. I just want to sleep all day with no interruptions.

"But with the ghost town stop, the tour won't be over

until almost midnight," Rand reminds me, worry filling his beautiful evergreen eyes. I reach over to touch his reddish-blond curls and smile.

"I know." I try not to smile at the thought of being free of Lucas and Angel for the entire day but my mouth keeps pulling upward.

"Promise you'll call me every hour," Rand demands.

"Can I sleep for a little bit first?" I ask, touched that he is so protective of me.

"God, you two are nauseating," Angel adds, tumbling off the chair, giving Rand and me a crotch shot on the way down.

"I'm proud of you, Angel. You're actually wearing underwear today." She sticks her tongue out at me.

"I could really care less about seeing some hole," Angel says, getting serious. After living with Angel for several months now at the Beta house I've realized that she talks a good game. She is just as worried about me as Rand is but wouldn't admit it for the world. This is her way of saying she wants to stay with me. With both of us being such powerful forces, our friendship is a delicate balance of her rarely admitting her true feelings and me never admitting that I already know them.

"I know a hole I'd like to see," Lucas jokes. We all ignore him because sometimes he is just too stupid for words.

"I really just want to be by myself to get some sleep," I beg, suddenly barely able to keep my eyes open. Rand winks at me, kisses my forehead, then gets off the bed and starts herding Lucas and Angel to the door.

"Sweet dreams, Aspen," I hear Rand say, right before the door clicks shut and I fall back to sleep.

I wake up four hours later feeling like a new girl. I spring out of bed and pull back the drapes to be welcomed with a breathtaking Las Vegas day. I can't believe that I am going to miss out on an entire day of vacation with Rand. I flop down on the bed and flip on the television. Maybe I can at least catch up on some pay-per-view.

"What is this crap?" I mutter to myself, going down the list of movies. They all seem to be in Spanish, not that you'd need much dialogue to figure out what is going on since they are all porn. I switch back to the local channels, which are filled with hotel channels trying to teach you how to gamble. I wouldn't mind learning how to be a rock star at blackjack, but what's the point when I can't even gamble?

"I can't believe this," I complain to absolutely no one as I stop on a local news station. A tiny woman with helmet hair is standing in front of Pirate's Cove shouting into her microphone. I turn up the volume hoping there isn't some sort of bomb threat at the hotel because I really don't want to run outside in my booty T-shirt.

"No, Phil. Apparently she left a note saying the pageant scene just wasn't for her and took off. So her mother doesn't suspect foul play. But it does leave the pageant officials in quite a quandary. For fifty years, the Miss Teen Queen competition has had a teen representative from all fifty states so this little girl has left some former queens with their tiaras in a bunch." She laughs. The screen pans back to the newscaster in the studio who is trying to keep a straight face. The on-scene reporter is still visible in a box on the top right hand of the screen. Highlighted in blue at the bottom of the screen the caption reads, "Miss Teen Queen Pageant Canceled?"

"The horror!" I shout in fake-outrage to my empty hotel room.

Miss Teen Queen wannabes are milling around, waving and striking poses, trying to get on live television.

"So what are officials going to do, Lorna?" the newscaster asks, clearly out of obligation.

"Well, Phil, they are really hoping that a beautiful teen girl between the ages of fifteen and twenty is watching and wants to fill this girl's shoes."

I groan, knowing that the hotel is going to be even more jam-packed with ditzy girls now.

"I should mention, Phil, that the girl who wants this honor has to be a resident of the state of Illinois," the reporter clarifies.

The remote control drops out of my hand at the same time my mouth flies open. That means Emerson is the girl who took off. Who knew a girl that used to be in 4-H could be so scandalous?

⊚

I take the shortest shower imaginable, barely stopping to cringe at the hotel's choice of complimentary shampoo and conditioner. I am going to be in need of serious professional hair help if I don't get my bag soon. I blow my hair out straight since I don't have any of my styling tools and Angel obviously doesn't believe in grooming. I dig through her makeup bag until I find some shades that don't make me look like I'm dressing up for Halloween. I have got to get Angel to the Clinique counter if it's the last thing I do.

I step out of the bathroom, still wrapped in a hotel towel, and I contemplate my choices. I can either A) do absolutely nothing and veg out in the room all day, B) put on my clothes from yesterday and hope I don't stink too bad, or C) venture into the scary depths of Angel's wardrobe. It takes all my resolve but I finally pull open the door to the armoire. Leopard prints jump out and threaten to blind me. I spot something green and yank it quickly out of the closet. It is a silk tank with a scoop neck. It is actually cute and I wonder for a second if the person who stayed here last left it behind to get victimized by Angel's brutal wardrobe. I pull a pair of dark jeans out of one of the drawers in the armoire. I hesitate, not wanting to face what is next, but finally I pull open the drawer containing Angel's underwear. A stack of rainbow-colored thongs stares back, openly mocking me. I deliberate about going caveman for a few seconds then pull a pink pair off the top. I get a jolt from a flashback of the last time I wore a thong: when I took down my ex-principal, Lulu Hott, partly by stashing a pocket knife in my thong when I went to her house to confront her. I can't stop myself from wondering if I might be in more danger right now, borrowing Angel's thong, than when I was trapped in Miss Hott's basement. I shake it off and slip into the borrowed clothes.

I'm surprised at how baggy Angel's clothes are—I always thought we were the exact same size—and then I remember the seafood incident. I need to get myself some sustenance before I start looking all Kate Moss. I'm probably totally dehydrated. I grab my Dooney, making sure I have my hotel key card, and am on my way to the lobby for a human-sized Coke, not that dinky crap the airline gives out, and maybe some Ben & Jerry's. Plus, I need to see what gossip I can dig up about Emerson. It's not like I have anything better to do. Besides, maybe there is something fishy going on. Ugh. My stomach rolls and it has nothing to do with Angel's thong. Yep, it's way too soon to be thinking about fish.

Three

Surprisingly, the lobby is nearly empty of Barbie clones. For a second, I wonder if they called the whole pageant off, but then a voluptuous redhead runs by with her cell phone plastered to her ear, saying something about being late for rehearsal. I dart into the lobby sundry store and grab a Coke. The clerk looks me up and down as I give her exact change and thank her.

"You're polite. You're not with the pageant, are you?" she asks, flipping through an issue of *US Weekly*.

"Oh, no way." I laugh. "Hey, do you know anything about the girl who quit the pageant?" I whisper, hoping to get a little insider information. I'll have all the scoop when my trio gets back.

"Just what they are saying on the news. That she left a note saying she didn't want to compete. I say good for her.

These competitions don't do anything but objectify women anyway," she says, frowning when she comes across an article about Jessica Simpson dumping her latest conquest. "She never should have left Nick," she mumbles.

"He's better off," I disagree. "So anyway, did you happen to see her before she took off?" I ask, trying to get her to focus.

"No, but her mom was in here this morning giving me some bull about how her credit card can't be rejected. I sorta felt bad for her but I gotta do what the machine tells me to," she says, pointing to the gray credit card processor.

Emerson's mom is obviously busted in the funds department. Emerson was competing in the pageant so that she could help her parents out financially. That much I know from what I overheard of her phone conversation. It doesn't make sense that she would just take off. Could evil forces possibly be at work here? I know I shouldn't even care, but Emerson is Lucas's friend so it's kind of like a two degrees of separation thing. I feel like I should at least poke around a bit. Emerson might be out in the big city all alone, and something tells me that 4-H never prepared her for that.

"Thanks for your help," I tell the clerk, popping the top on my Coke and guzzling half of it down. The fizzy goodness revitalizes me and I make my way to the lobby.

"Thirsty?" a middle-aged man with greasy, slicked-back hair and an outdated polyester suit asks. I hate it when old men try to strike up a conversation with me. It's kind of sad how they don't have a clue how disgusting they really are and how they believe that a girl my age might still be attracted to them. UGH!

"No," I reply, when he continues to stare me down for an answer. I breeze by him, holding my breath to avoid suffocating on his gag-worthy cologne. He starts to give me a dirty look but is quickly led away by a hotel employee. He's probably not the only pervert hanging out at Pirate's Cove hoping to snag himself a trophy wife.

I head to the front desk to find out what room Emerson was staying in. I figure the best way to find out what really happened to her is to retrace her steps, starting with her hotel room. The male clerk is amazingly easy to convince that I'm a long-lost niece of Mrs. Chambers and willingly gives me her room number. I jump on the elevator and ride up to Emerson's floor. I bang softly on the door, hoping her mother is still here.

The door flings open and Mrs. Chambers's face falls when she sees it is just me standing there. She obviously thought Emerson had come to her senses and returned. I feel sort of horrible.

"I'm sorry to bother you, Mrs. Chambers. I'm Lucas's friend Aspen Brooks. I was just wondering if I could ask you a few questions?"

"Of course, Aspen. Come right in," she says, holding the door open wider so I can move inside. She wipes a tear with the back of her hand and shuts the door.

I move inside the room and take a seat on one of the made beds. The room doesn't look like I would imagine a beauty contestant's room to look. It is neat with very few personal items. I notice a beat-up gray suitcase in the corner of the room with a hot pink Miss Teen Queen tag attached to it. How strange that Emerson wouldn't take her suitcase with her.

"I'm really sorry about Emerson," I say, not knowing exactly where to start to pry some information out of Mrs. Chambers.

"This just isn't like her. I mean, I thought it was strange that she even wanted to enter this beauty pageant, but I went along with it. Emerson has never been one for getting all dolled up," she tells me as if this fact isn't totally obvious. "All my girl cares about is milking the cows on time and showing her horses." Mrs. Chambers breaks down sobbing into her press-on-nails-covered hands.

"What about the note?" I ask, trying to hide the excitement in my voice. I hate to admit it but I've become a real detective junkie. It's not really my fault. I mean, I stumbled onto two missing persons cases in the last eighteen months and solved them both, risking life, limb, and Dooney, both times. Now I'm hooked. It is going to be kind of a buzzkill if I have to admit that Emerson walked away of her own accord.

"Here it is," Mrs. Chambers says, passing me a handwritten note on hotel stationery. I curse myself for not signing up for a handwriting analysis class last summer, which could have helped me figure out if Emerson was under duress while penning this note.

"Does anything in here seem strange to you?" I ask, scanning the boring note. Emerson just apologizes and says she wants to help the family by not being a burden anymore.

"No, not really. I'm so worried about her. This is a dangerous city and Emerson isn't a city-savvy girl," she says, getting up and sliding open the closet door. She lifts the beat-up suitcase onto the bed and starts folding and placing clothes inside.

"Did you call the police?" I ask. She nods her head wearily.

I can already imagine the spiel they gave her before she even tells me a word. The fuzz and their stupid policy about how a person has to be missing for twenty-four hours before they can file a report. Luckily for Mrs. Chambers, I don't have to adhere to the same rigid guidelines as the black-and-whites.

"Are you going somewhere?"

"I can't afford to stay here anymore," she says, averting her eyes. I feel so sorry for her. First her daughter takes off, and then she gets her credit card declined. She pulls a familiar pink T-shirt off a hanger and starts folding it.

"Hey, let me see that," I say. She turns the shirt around and I immediately recognize the John Deere insignia on the front. Emerson was wearing it last night and I would almost bet that for a country girl like Emerson, this shirt is her signature item.

"How often does she wear that shirt?" I ask, getting excited.

"Oh, it's her favorite. She even washed it in the sink last night so she could wear it again this week," Mrs. Chambers answers sadly, delicately placing the shirt into Emerson's suitcase.

"I knew it," I exclaim, startling Mrs. Chambers. "If Emerson was going to take off on her own, do you really think she would leave behind her signature item?" That would be like me taking off without my Dooney. The thought alone gives me shivers. Mrs. Chambers gives me a confused look.

"Okay, what exactly is missing?" I ask her. She goes through the closet, dictating a checklist.

"All that is gone is a simple black cocktail dress that she was going to wear for the judges' interview," she answers, looking puzzled. I can't help but crack a small smile as I realize that I have a new case to investigate.

☺

Where in the world could Emerson be? I'm on my way to the concierge desk to ask if there is a rodeo in town when my cell phone rings with Rand's personal ring tone, "I Wanna Be Your Lover."

"Hi, sweetie. How's the hole?" I ask sweetly, dying to tell him the news.

"Lucas and Angel are driving me insane," he says, sounding grouchy. "They are fighting so much that I can't even hear the damn tour guide." He sighs in defeat.

"What are they fighting about now?" I ask, totally pissed that they are ruining the only thing Rand cared about doing on his vacation.

"Same stuff. Angel wants to get married and Lucas doesn't."

"What? She acted like she dropped all of that crazy business last night. You just wait until I get a hold of her."

"Can you imagine if the two of them got married?" He laughs.

"Yeah, like where are they going to live? The sorority house? Those two are a trip. So anyway, Emerson disappeared and I'm going to solve the case," I blurt out, knowing that Rand is going to be so unthrilled and hoping by getting it out there really fast he won't notice.

"Excuse me? When I last left you, you were delirious and smelled like puke. Exactly when did you feel good enough to tie on your girl detective cape?" he asks, slightly irritated.

"I woke up feeling so much better and had to come down to get something to drink. The place was buzzing with the news. Of course, they are all amateurs and they just thought that Emerson went AWOL from the pageant.

But I figured out the truth. Well, kind of," I admit, since I don't officially have any clues about what happened to Emerson yet.

I hear a loud voice from Rand's end announcing that the bus is getting ready to leave.

"Shit. Aspen, this isn't Comfort. There are some really dangerous people in Las Vegas. Promise me you'll get the cops involved and not do anything stupid on your own."

"I was just getting ready to call the cops," I say, not totally lying since I was thinking about calling my friend Detective Harry Malone to get his opinion. Not that he is usually right, but I thought I'd give him the benefit of the doubt. Plus, he's almost two thousand miles away so he can't really interfere.

"Aspen, promise me you won't get yourself into anything," Rand says, more forceful this time.

"I promise," I say, crossing my fingers.

"You'd better not be crossing your fingers either," he says, nailing me. "I'll be back in seven hours. Just behave yourself until then. I love you."

"I love you too, Rand," I say, meaning every word.

☙

"So you've got nothing?" I ask, irritated.

"Aspen, I'm two thousand miles away. How am I supposed to know if this pageant girl has disappeared or just walked away?" Detective Harry Malone yells, not happy that I'm interrupting his workday. Like Comfort, Illinois, is such a hotbed of criminal activity. He's probably just swamped with stolen bike cases.

Harry and I have a messed-up sort of history. I first met him when he was working the case of the Beauty Bandit. When my mom became a victim, Harry became an unwanted and very unfollically challenged staple around our house. We got closer when he kind of saved me, Angel, and my mom from certain death by glue gun at the hand of my ex-principal, Lulu Hott. Then last semester Harry and his guys busted into my ex-sorority house just as I was solving another crime. Harry is what my dad would describe as a day late and a dollar short, but he's a good guy and I trust him when I'm in a bind.

"Can't you call somebody? Don't you have any contacts or anything?" I whine.

"Not everything is like *CSI*, Aspen," Harry grumbles.

"Oh, just forget it. I'll handle it myself," I say, knowing this will get him.

"Just a minute. Let me put in a call. I'll have a detective contact you. Don't go doing anything stupid, Aspen," Harry says, before he clicks off. He's got these total surrogate dad feelings for me so I know he wouldn't want me going off to investigate by myself. Once I explain my hunch to the Las Vegas detective, I'll hand the case off to them and resume my much-needed R & R.

"This is really nice of you to let me stay in your room. Are you sure your roommate won't mind?" Mrs. Chambers says, scooting her suitcases into a corner of our hotel room.

"Angel is a really giving individual and I know that she'll be happy to help out any friend of Lucas's," I say, lying through my teeth. It serves Angel right for acting like she was over the whole getting hitched thing then going behind my back.

"Just make yourself comfortable, Mrs. Chambers. The detective should be here soon."

"Please, call me Mona," she says, sitting down in the chair that I was sure Lucas and Angel had broken.

"Okay, Mona. Has anything strange happened since you got here?" I ask, hoping to find even a shred of evidence that could help figure out what happened to Emerson.

"You mean besides the parade of baby prostitutes downstairs?" She laughs.

"Why did you let Emerson be in the pageant if you felt that way?" I ask, confused.

"She was very insistent. I have a feeling that she was hoping to win the prize money to help out her father and me," she admits, wringing her hands. "Our farm is in foreclosure." Her cheeks get splotchy from embarrassment.

"Everybody has hard times, Mona. That's nothing to be embarrassed about." I completely sympathize with her.

I remember how scared I was that I'd have to spend the rest of my life shopping at TJ Maxx when I found out how much money my mom had racked up in credit card debt.

"I don't even care about the farm. I just want to find my daughter," Mona sobs.

I reach over to comfort her just as I hear a knock on the door.

"We'll get it figured out," I say, rushing to let in the detective.

☺

It's almost like she is trying to make herself look ugly on purpose. The female detective, that is. She is sitting on my bed reading the note Emerson left behind. Her face is scrunched up like she is having a hard time reading Emerson's loopy scrawl even though she is wearing tortoiseshell glasses circa 1989. Her mousy brown hair, which is streaked with some bits of gray, is pulled back into a sloppy ponytail. Not a sloppy-in-a-sexy-way ponytail, but sloppy in an I'm-too-lazy-to-even-brush-my-hair way. She is wearing wrinkled khaki pants, a blue button-down shirt, and clunky brown lace-up shoes. She does have a good base: high cheekbones and large, almond-shaped eyes. If only I had my makeup bag. Damn airline.

"Hey, do you have any pull with Vegas Now? They lost my bag," I ask, figuring it's worth a try. Detective

Grant looks up from the note and throws me a not-so-subtle dirty look. Well, excuse me!

"What leads you to believe that Miss Chambers was involved in some sort of foul play?" she asks Mona.

"Aspen thought it seemed suspicious that she left without taking her pink John Deere T-shirt."

Detective Grant looks back toward me and openly snickers. Forget the makeover, I want to give her two black eyes.

"I understand that you fancy yourself quite the little girl detective," Detective Grant says, standing and handing the note back to Mona.

"I don't fancy myself anything. I just know that I've solved a missing person's case and helped apprehend a serial kidnapper. You can call it what you want. I just know that I've got good instincts and I sense that something happened to Emerson," I say, hating that I'm defending myself to someone who doesn't even moisturize.

"Right," she answers back sarcastically. "Well, I've been working cases since you were still in Pampers and I say the girl just walked away. She obviously didn't want to compete in the pageant. Maybe she was feeling inferior to the other girls and couldn't handle it."

Mona suppresses a gasp. I really want to throw down with this chick right now but I'm afraid that some of her ugly might actually rub off on me. I can't believe this is who Harry sent to follow up on Emerson's case.

"That is the lamest explanation ever. Emerson was

practically a shoo-in to win," I shout, my voice trembling because I'm furious that she isn't taking this seriously. If only Harry had some jurisdiction in Las Vegas, he would trust any instinct that I had.

"I see it every year. Some girls just can't handle the pressure of being onstage in front of the whole world." She smiles smugly.

"Whatever," I smart off, knowing I'm not getting anywhere with her. I eyeball Mona, trying to get her to contribute something but she just sits there staring at the note.

"I never should have let her compete. I put the weight of our debt on her tiny shoulders," Mona sobs.

"Great. Now look what you did," I whisper to the detective.

"I'm sure she'll come back in a few days after she's calmed down, Mrs. Chambers," Detective Grant offers halfheartedly.

"I guess I'm on my own, as usual," I say. I can't believe she doesn't even offer to review the surveillance tapes from the hotel the night Emerson disappeared. As much as I hate to stereotype, I'm starting to believe all the doughnut chatter I've heard about cops.

"Let me give you a little advice, Miss Brooks," she says, getting right up in my face. "Minding your own business while you are in my city would be advisable." She stomps to the door, then stops to turn around and glare at me, giving me just enough time to get in the last word, which I totally heart.

"I've got some advice of my own, Detective Grant. A little lip gloss wouldn't kill you," I yell as she lets the door slam behind her. Take that, you fashion-challenged beyotch. Now I have one more reason to solve this mystery—to prove to Detective Plain Jane that I can do it. I have a hunch that Detective Grant might not be completely convinced that Emerson walked away either, but she doesn't want to go pissing off the city officials, her police department, or the sponsors of the Miss Teen Queen Pageant by letting it get out that a young girl disappeared. Too bad she doesn't know that I've practically got Nancy Grace on my speed dial. Sorry, Detective Grant. When Aspen Brooks is in Vegas, nothing stays secret in Vegas.

☺

I spend the next fifteen minutes consoling Mona. I'm seriously regretting telling her she could stay in my room. I have to plan my next move and I don't have time to sit around babysitting her. I'd like to have this whole mystery figured out before Rand and the couple from hell gets back from their dam tour. I've never solved a mystery that fast but I like to set high goals for myself.

"I can't help thinking that the pageant has something to do with this. I'm going to start by interviewing some of the girls," I say, checking myself in the mirror to make sure I still look presentable. As shocking as it is to see myself in Angel's ensemble, I look positively adorable.

"Wait a minute. I've got an idea." Mona pops up, looking excited. Finally she is becoming a little more proactive in helping find her daughter. I nod for her to continue while running my lip-gloss applicator over my lips. Thank goodness I always keep spare lip gloss in my Dooney.

"You could take Emerson's spot in the pageant," Mona exclaims, looking proud of herself.

I nearly jab the applicator down my throat at the thought, then I remember the first rule that any good detective has to follow: Sometimes you have to sacrifice yourself for your case. Designer ball gowns, Christian Louboutin heels, satin sashes, armfuls of roses, and sparkly tiaras. Now those are some sacrifices I'm willing to make, but this week is supposed to be about relaxing with Rand. I want to help Mona out as much as I can but if I enter the pageant, it will take up all my time.

"Mona, I'm flattered . . ." My cell phone rings, interrupting the delicate letdown I was in the process of giving Mona. I hold my index finger up to signal her to hold on.

Lucas's cell phone number flashes on my display.

"Aspen, is it really true that Emerson is missing?" Lucas asks in a frantic voice.

"Lucas, calm down. She left a note. I'm sure she's fine," I lie.

"She wouldn't do this, Aspen. She wouldn't run off and worry her family. Something is wrong. You have to help her, Aspen," he pleads.

There are only a few times in Lucas's relationship with me that I have heard him this desperate. I think back to his ass-backward scheme of voting Rand the homecoming king our senior year. Even though Lucas was dating me, he knew that Rand and I belonged together. Of course he was hitting Angel on the side but I've always believed there was a tiny piece of altruism involved in his gesture.

The bottom line is that Lucas is one of my closest friends. And a friend asking me for my help is my Kryptonite.

Look out, Miss Teen Queen, here comes Aspen Brooks.

Four

"Oh my goodness. She's perfect," the lady in charge of the pageant squeals, while playing with my hair. As much as I love her compliment, I still bat her hand away. I want to launch into a spiel about how many oils are on the human hand at any one time and how quickly just a few tugs could wreak havoc on my blown-out locks, but instead I just flash her my pearlies. She comes off as nice but my creep meter is on high alert for some reason. I subtly step back so she can't soil my locks any more than she already has.

"I want her to take Emerson's place in the pageant." Mona beams.

The pageant director, a slight woman who stands eye level with my chest, raises both her arms in jubilation and practically starts jumping for joy. "This is wonderful. I thought we were going to have to cancel the pageant when we couldn't find an Illinois resident to take Emerson's place," she says, wiping invisible sweat from her brow. "You are an Illinois resident, aren't you?" she asks hesitantly.

"Absolutely," I state proudly, digging my license out of my Dooney and flashing it at her.

"You are going to have a lot of catching up to do, Miss Aspen. The girls have been practicing their routines all week. This isn't some cheesy county fair competition," she says snidely.

"What kind of routines?" I ask suspiciously, choosing to ignore what I'm sure is a dig at the kind of pageants she assumes we have in Comfort.

Her eyes seem to glaze over as she mentally pictures the routines. "Those are top secret."

Um, okay. Something tells me that the Botox toxins in this lady's face are starting to seep into her bloodstream. Obviously I won't have clearance to receive the top-secret dance moves until she deems me acceptable for the pageant. Whatever. It's not like I can't dance or something.

I start to feel dizzy as images of jazz hands and stepball changes leap through my mind. I shiver at the last image of a little girl in a pink leotard looking quite pathetic as she tries to plié through the air and ends up eating the dance floor. I wonder where that image came from? I mean,

I've watched *Dancing with the Stars* just like everybody else, but I've never had formal dance training. What am I saying? Could I actually be doubting myself? As if! I'm a quick learner and this dance routine business is going to be a cakewalk.

"I can handle it," I say, interrupting her chatter about the end routine featuring live animals. I shake it off hoping that I don't suffer a Siegfried & Roy, well, just Roy I guess, fate.

"What's your talent?" she asks me, and I glance, terrified, at Mona. Talent? I have to pick just one?

"Um . . ." I say, completely at a loss, which never happens.

"Aspen would like to keep her talent a secret until she becomes more familiar with the other girls," Mona says, saving me.

"Okay, but I'll need to know by curtain time," she says, thrusting a clipboard at me. On it is a questionnaire that asks things like my favorite music, food, hobbies, and goals. I walk over to a couch in the lobby to fill it out. Mona stays put, talking to the pageant director, who is suddenly flocked by thirty girls claiming that there has been some sort of swimwear emergency.

Mona sits down beside me just as I finish filling out the questionnaire. She pulls out her cell phone and checks the screen. Defeated, she closes the phone and stuffs it back into her purse. I feel so bad for her. At first, I think it's just because she is carrying a fake Coach purse, but then I remember that she has no idea what has happened to her favorite person in the whole world. I would freak in a big way if anything ever happened to Rand.

"I'm going to get this figured out for you," I promise her, touching her arm.

"You are a very determined girl, and I believe if anyone can, it will be you," she says, giving me a halfhearted smile. "I'm going to make myself useful and search for Emerson on the Strip. I'll catch up with you later. Good luck," she says, wandering out of the hotel looking like a puppy that just got kicked.

I get up and hand the clipboard back to the pageant director whose name tag, I just noticed, reads Andrea.

"Move it, we're burning daylight," Andrea says harshly. Her whole demeanor seems to have changed with Mona gone. Now seems like a perfect time to establish some boundaries and let her know that just because I'm participating in this little pageant of hers, she is so not the boss of me.

"Actually, Andrea, I need some time to go get myself some clothes to rehearse in. All my bags were lost and this is all I have." I gesture to my outfit.

"You need to address me as 'Pageant Mistress.' And you've got twenty minutes," she spouts in disgust.

Pageant Mistress? She has got to be joking. But she isn't cracking a smile. I ignore her and turn on my heel. I'm all about solving this mystery but I'm not all about getting bossed around by some sadistic Barbie wannabe who probably harbors issues of resentment for not being cute enough to ever enter a pageant herself. Okay, so that was mean, but I've had kind of a crappy spring break so far. And twenty minutes to find comfortable, yet trendy clothes to rehearse in? That is so not happening. Pageant Mistress will see me when she sees me and she is just going to have to deal. I disappear out of Pirate's Cove and onto the Strip for some retail therapy.

☺

Thank goodness for emergency credit cards. I don't take credit lightly with the mess my mom got us in, to the tune of thousands of dollars' worth of debt, but sometimes credit cards can be real lifesavers. Besides, I'm totally going to send LVPD a bill after I solve their case. Armed with the most adorable Burberry bikini and matching heels, matching pink spandex sports bra and workout shorts and ballet slippers to practice in, I head back to the hotel. Mona said that I could borrow Emerson's costumes for all the dance routines so now all I am missing is a formal gown. I'll have to send Angel, with a list of intricate details, to hunt down the perfect dress for me.

☺

"You're what?" Rand practically screams into the phone. I hold my cell phone away from my delicate eardrum and don't put it back until I'm sure he is done having his little hissy fit.

"I'm helping Emerson's mom by taking Emerson's place in the pageant," I repeat, already holding the phone away from my ear in case he blows up again.

"But this was supposed to be our vacation. You promised you would just relax," he whines.

"I can't help it, Rand. A girl is missing and no one is taking this seriously. How can you expect me to just walk away from that?" I spout, getting a little pissy myself.

"So the truth comes out. You aren't entering the pageant to help Mrs. Chambers. You are trying to get the backstage scoop on the pageant girls." He laughs sarcastically.

"Maybe . . . which will in turn help me solve this mystery. Which helps Mona," I say, delighted that I have managed, once again, to justify my actions.

"Mona, huh?" Rand replies in a more subdued fashion. "So you really think somebody took this girl?"

"I know she wouldn't walk away from her family when they need her most. I have to do this, Rand. She's Lucas's friend."

"Okay." He sighs. "I don't like it, but the pageant is only one night, so how much time can it possibly take up?"

It never ceases to amaze me how simple boys can be. How can they not realize the time that goes into getting beautiful? Not to mention learning two choreographed dances, practicing my runway walk, perfecting my interview answers . . . and that doesn't even include all the time I'll have to spend bonding with my fellow contestants. But I don't have the energy to explain all of this to Rand right now. Besides, Pageant Mistress is flapping her hands at me so fast that I'm pretty sure she's about to lift off.

"Rand, I've got to get going. I'll see you when you get back," I say, rushing to get off the phone.

"Just one more thing, Aspen. Lucas and Angel broke up," he says, just as I click off because psycho Pageant Mistress is reaching for my phone. I throw my phone into my purse and throw her a look that says she better not even think about putting her filthy paws on my Dooney.

"We need you onstage. Yesterday," she huffs, stomping off, causing quite a scene in the middle of the hotel lobby. So much for the sweet-as-honey woman who was thrilled that I was saving her pageant. I reluctantly follow her with Rand's final words buzzing in my ears. Lucas and Angel broke up? Who breaks up on spring break? Only those two brain donors. Great, now I have another problem to deal with. This vacation is turning out to be a lot of work.

⊙

"Girls, this is Aspen. She's going to be filling the vacancy of Miss Illinois since Emerson took off. Autumn, introduce her to everyone," Pageant Mistress says, rather hatefully.

I'm tempted to tell her that Emerson is the victim here and she should not be bad-mouthing a victim, but she kind of scares me. An adorable redhead with a sloppy pageboy haircut bounds up and shakes my hand while all the other girls just gawk at me like I have a unibrow.

"Hi, Aspen. Welcome aboard," she says genuinely. "Okay, I'm just going to give you a short rundown of who won't shred your clothes," she whispers into my ear. I stifle a laugh. Autumn points to a pint-sized Latina girl who can't be over four feet tall.

"This is Marisa. She's Miss California," Autumn says, loud enough for Marisa to hear. She turns and smiles at me but her grin doesn't match the angry look in her eyes. I turn to Autumn, confused, because I thought she was going to point out the nice girls first. "Oh, she just doesn't have her eyebrows drawn on yet. She's harmless."

Relieved, I give Marisa a half-wave. I notice a beautiful girl standing next to her who reminds me of Jennifer Hudson with less junk in her trunk. She is dressed in a pink tank top and matching shorts but is wearing white gloves.

"That's Catrina, Miss Arizona. She's going to be a hand model if the whole pageant circuit doesn't work out," Autumn says, which explains the gloves. I try not to crack up as I wave to her. She smiles at me but doesn't lift one of her precious hands in a wave.

"Those are the Dakota twins. They aren't really twins but they're joined at the hip so we just call them that."

The blonde and brunette seem to be comparing chest

sizes as they stand next to each other and push their boobs out. I bite my lip to suppress a laugh.

"They are harmless but they won't be up for Mensa memberships anytime soon," Autumn clarifies, as if it is actually needed.

I realize that a crowd of blondes is making its way toward me. One girl with huge hair, who seems to be the leader, falls back. She seems to examine me from head to toe, wearing a scowl the whole time.

"And here are the ones who will shred your clothes. We call them the trophy wives," Autumn whispers, getting crowded out by the blondes. "Because that's what they'll become when they are too old for pageants."

The blondes swallow me up in a peroxide, collagen, silicone bubble. They offer hugs, arm squeezes, and words of encouragement. I want to tell them that I wasn't born yesterday and that I know they'll be praying I break out in hives the night of the competition, but I just smile back. I've already decided to get a locked case for my clothes and makeup, fearing I'll suffer a pepper spray fate like Miss Puerto Rico. That crap is so bad for my asthma (which I found out the hard way by accidentally spraying myself last semester when I was trying to deal with some pesky rodents). If I didn't know better, I'd think these girls were actually nice, and not threatened by me at all, that's how good they are. I smile at them and start to back out of the circle they've created around me, fearing claustrophobia might kick in any minute.

"Okay, enough touchy-feely time. Back to work. We have to get Aspen up to speed on all of our routines and we only have forty-eight hours," Pageant Mistress says, prompting all the girls to rush into their places onstage.

"What should I do?" I ask, feeling strangely out of my element.

"Just watch for now and then when you feel like you've got some of the routine down, go ahead and join in," she says hurriedly, rushing backstage to turn on some music. The Elvis song "Rubbernecking" comes blaring through unseen speakers. The girls dazzle me with their sophisticated, perfectly in-sync moves. I stand off to the side of the stage, watching them intensely. As nervous as I'm feeling about learning all these dance moves, I'm also excited to think that Rand will be able to sit in the crowd and watch me perform. That is definitely going to be a perk of this investigation. I pick up on the fact that the dance only really has eight different moves but endless combinations. I should be able to master this routine in no time. I stifle a laugh watching the girls do this weird neck move that makes them look like turkeys. I'm sure it will look really cool with our costumes on though. I imagine the costumes for this dance to be glittery dresses made out of sequins that swirl around our knees every time we spin to the music.

"Join in anytime, Brooks," Pageant Mistress yells impatiently.

I drop my purse and leap onto the dance floor, energized by the music. I scoot up next to Autumn. She looks over and grins at me attempting to copy her moves. The routine is harder than it looks and I get mixed up quite a bit, but I'm a quick learner so I'm not even worried about it. I'm caught in mid-step when the music cuts off.

"Where exactly did you learn how to dance? The School for the Rhythmically Challenged?" Pageant Mistress asks, laughing. A few smirks come up from the back row until I throw an evil look their way.

"That's very funny. It's my first time and I'm doing the best I can," I say, trying to keep a lid on my temper.

"If that's your best, that's really scary. You need to step it up or I'm going to have to rethink you being in the pageant." Her words sting, and tears spring to my eyes. I'm hungry, tired, and probably dehydrated, which is making me off my game. Normally I wouldn't bat an eye at this beyotch's comments but today they are really getting under my skin. I should just cut my losses and head to the Forum Shops. Why should I care about what happened to some girl I don't know anyway?

The image of Lucas's crushed face, as I tell him that I would rather go shopping at Caesars than help his friend, flashes through my mind. Crap! Sometimes my loyalty to my besties is such a disability.

"I could help her," Autumn pipes up.

"I don't think the entire cast of *Dancing with the*

Stars could help her, but, Autumn, if you want to give it a try, be my guest. Everybody else is dismissed for the night and should meet back here at six A.M."

Everyone skitters out of the auditorium except me and Autumn.

"Am I really that bad?" I ask, bracing myself for the answer.

"It just takes some practice. You'll get it," Autumn replies, then starts explaining the routine step-by-step in detail.

⊙

Two hours and three blisters later, Autumn and I walk out of the auditorium together.

"Can I buy you a mocktail or something for helping me?" I ask, hobbling along.

"That would be great, but I'll have to cut it short to get some beauty sleep," she jokes, even though now that we are in the harsher light of the lobby, I can see that she doesn't need any sleep to be beautiful. To my amazement she bounds along on endless legs acting like she didn't just rehearse the whole day. I practically need a walker.

"Let's go here," I say, pointing to the first café that comes along. A waitress seats us and we both order a fruit juice spritzer. I add a cheeseburger and fries to my order as Autumn regards me with caution.

"You're not bulimic, are you?" she asks with wide eyes.

"Oh, gross. As if," I say, sliding my feet out of my shoes. I know I should be focusing on whether Autumn knows anything about Emerson, but all I can think about right now is some antibiotic ointment and a couple of Band-Aids.

"Sorry. You just never know with some of these girls. So far I've counted two bulimics, one cutter, one rehab escapee, and I'm pretty sure that Miss Mississippi has a bun in the oven," she whispers.

I'm stunned. Not by the rundown of dysfunctional pageant contestants, but because I totally lucked out and befriended the most observant girl here. She is so going to help me figure out what happened to Emerson.

"I guess we all have our issues, huh?" I laugh, taking a sip of my drink.

"I'm sorry. I didn't mean to say it that way. It's just being quarantined with the same people all day is starting to get to me a bit. I already miss Emerson," she says, tucking her hair behind her ears.

"So you and Emerson were friends?" I prod, looking away so that I don't seem too eager for her answer.

"She seemed to be the only other one here that wasn't out for just the tiara. She was here because she needed the money for her family, just like I need it for college."

"It seems kind of weird that she would just take off like that," I say.

"You probably won't think so after you rehearse with us for an entire day." She laughs, not exactly giving me the answer I was hoping for.

"Did Emerson have any enemies?" I ask, taking a more direct approach.

She takes a long sip of her drink and seems to consider my question. I see her nodding and I have to contain my excitement at the thought that I might be getting my first real tip.

"It's a beauty pageant. Aren't we all enemies?" she asks, getting up from the table.

"I guess so," I agree, remembering how just eighteen months ago, Angel and I would have torn each other to shreds over a tiara, and there wasn't even any money involved.

"Thanks for the drink, Aspen," she says, turning to go.

"Hey, Autumn," I say, touching her arm. She turns and smiles at me. "Am I really that bad?"

Her entire demeanor shifts but she tries to keep a smile on her face. She ends up looking like a demented clown. "We'll work on it together," she says, bolting out of the café.

How can this be? Surely she's mistaken. I'm good at everything. I bite into my cheeseburger while trying to dig up a memory that could prove Autumn wrong. I'm on my third bite when I remember dancing with Rand at prom. We were so good that people backed up and made a circle around us, just to watch. I sigh as I shove a handful of fries in my mouth. I knew there was no way Autumn could be right.

"There's my girl," Rand says, plopping down in the chair where Autumn was sitting. It is amazing how the very sight of him automatically makes everything right in my world again. My feet don't hurt anymore. I'm a fabulous dancer, and I am so going to find Lucas's tomboy friend. Right after I make out with my boyfriend a little bit. I throw down some money, drag Rand out of the café, and sequester us in an elevator.

He doesn't blink an eye when I push the button for the highest floor. I wrap one arm over one of his perfectly filled out shoulders, and my other arm goes behind his head. I put my hand in his hair and pull him into my lips. Our tongues automatically know which way to go to drive the other crazy. Rand grabs my butt and hoists me onto his hips. I wrap my legs around his waist, then start kissing his neck. He leans his head back against the mirror-faced elevator wall, a smile playing on his delectable lips.

I start to kiss him again when Pageant Mistress's voice pops into my head. Talk about a buzzkill. I have to fix this dance issue once and for all. I'll ask the one person in the whole world that I know would never lie to me.

"Rand?" I whisper into his ear.

"Eh?" he answers, clearly out of his mind with desire for me.

"You wouldn't ever lie to me, would you?" I say, already knowing the answer.

"Never, Aspen," he says, trying to lose himself in my lips again. I pull back a bit so I can get my answer.

"Am I a good dancer?" I whisper.

"Oh, Aspen. Why did you have to go there?" he says, dropping my legs back to the elevator floor and sighing heavily.

Crap. So it really is true. There is something I'm not good at.

Five

"But when we danced at prom, everybody backed up so they could admire us," I say, still unwilling to admit that I could possibly be rhythmically challenged.

"They were backing up because they were afraid you were going to lose a heel and somebody was going to get knocked out," Rand replies, cracking up.

"This isn't funny. Do you know that I have to learn two dance routines and perform them in front of the whole world?" I am stressing out beyond belief. "I was already worried that I'll slip and fall during the evening gown portion of the competition. Do you realize that Miss USA has fallen two consecutive years at the Miss Universe Pageant? The odds are not exactly stacked in my favor, especially with this new information coming to light that obviously I'm lucky to even be able to walk upright."

"No offense, but I don't think the whole world watches the Miss Teen Queen Pageant," Rand offers, failing to be helpful.

"Whatever," I mutter, too exhausted to start spouting viewing stats on the pageant, which I totally know. While the adult pageant is consistently losing viewers and having a hard time finding a station to sponsor it, the teen version is all the rage. I heard that it has something to do with the growing superficiality of my generation, but I just think it's because girls my age like to get dressed up and wear tiaras. Why does everything always have to have a deep and meaningful answer? Can't playing dress-up just be enough? Jeez.

Rand and I step off the elevator onto the floor where Angel and I are staying. We are both shocked to see a distraught-looking Angel curled up in a ball by the door of our hotel room.

"I haven't had a chance to fill you in about the breakup yet," Rand whispers, gesturing to Angel. I roll my eyes at him, still not believing that anyone in their right mind would break up on spring break.

"Angel, what are you doing on the floor?" I ask.

She pulls herself up, which seems to take every ounce of energy she has. Her jet-black hair is matted to her head and her normally heavily made-up face is bare except for her red-rimmed eyes.

"Oh, Aspen. It's horrible. Lucas and I broke up," she moans, throwing herself into my arms.

I roll my eyes at Rand, who is holding back a chuckle at Angel's melodramatics. I squeeze her tightly then pat her on the back to let her know I seriously need my personal space back.

"Who broke up with who?" I ask, once she has regained a tiny bit of composure.

"Lucas didn't want to get married so I had no choice but to end it," she answers, wiping away tear remnants from her cheeks.

"Why in the name of everything that is holy would you want to marry Lucas?" I ask, scared to hear the answer. Okay, so Lucas isn't a total nightmare. He actually has moments of true sweetness, but we are talking about a guy who has decided to talk like a pirate for the duration of our vacation. He's got the maturity level of a gnat. Not exactly matrimonial material.

"Because I love him and I'm ready to make a lifelong commitment," she says, tearing up again. "But obviously he doesn't feel the same way."

"Of course he loves you or he wouldn't put up with all your crap. But getting married at nineteen is just crazy. You guys don't have any money. You aren't done with school. You haven't done anything yet. Why would you want to tie yourself down?" I ask, trying to reason with her.

"You sound just like Lucas. Does everything always have to be so practical? Can't love just win out every once in a while?"

I sigh, too tired to deal with this right now. I look to

Rand for help but he is glancing around like he is about to make a run for it. In his defense, I guess he did put up with this drama all day today on the dam tour.

"We'll figure it out tomorrow, Angel. Why don't you get some sleep?" I say, practically pleading.

"Because the cow-patty thrower's mom is in my bed. What the hell have you been doing today?" she demands, suddenly forgetting all about her troubled love life.

Rand leans down, kisses my cheek, then says good night. As soon as he disappears into the elevator, my feet hurt again, Angel is staring me down for an answer, and I'm realizing that I have to share my bed with a stranger. How do I get myself into these things?

☺

Five A.M. comes very early, especially since Angel kept me up until the middle of the night discussing her tragic breakup with Lucas. I sneak out of bed, careful not to wake Mona—not like the dead could with the way the woman snores—and take a quick shower. I slip into my workout clothes, throw my wet hair into a ponytail (which is the ultimate hair no-no), and slip downstairs.

I grab a bagel slathered with cream cheese and a bottle of OJ from the café downstairs and trot into the auditorium. I'm feeling surprisingly energized as I've decided that I am going to beat this rhythmically challenged thing. I'm going to practice so hard and totally have the routines down. I'm going to be the star of the show. The belle of the ball. The . . .

"It's about freakin' time, princess," evil Pageant Mistress yells at me, almost causing me to choke on my bagel.

"What? You said six. It's six," I mumble through my last bite of bagel, pointing to the clock.

"It's six-oh-one," she grumbles, then stomps offstage.

"Is she always such an uber-hag?" I ask Autumn, stashing my OJ offstage.

"Pretty much." She laughs. She looks entirely too perky in her purple sports bra and tennis skirt. She even has her hair done and makeup on. I almost feel second rate next to her. Almost.

"I'm going to do a lot better today," I tell her, hoping the positive mantra will make it all the way down to my feet.

"I'm sure you will," she says, smiling back confidently.

"It doesn't matter. You still aren't going to win," a hateful voice says from behind me.

"Excuse you?" I say, spinning on my ballet-shoed heel. My face practically gets buried in an overabundance of cleavage. I glance up to see the head leading the boobs. Bloodred collagenized lips scowl down at me. I glance farther up to icy blue eyes attempting to bore holes in me topped off with a blond Amy Winehouse do.

"Miss Texas, I presume," I ask her breasts, jokingly, referring to the size of her hair. Autumn fake coughs to hide a giggle.

"You aren't going to be laughing when I completely

humiliate you in front of the entire world," the evil blonde says, stalking off.

"Who's the Anna Nicole knockoff?" I ask Autumn as we skitter to take our places as the music starts.

"She's the offspring of that," she answers back, pointing to Pageant Mistress, before seamlessly segueing into the first routine.

I'm stunned, which causes me to immediately miss a beat, but I quickly catch up. It takes all my concentration to stay focused on the steps and I have to push any thoughts of beauty pageants hindered by nepotism, missing girls, or broken-up friends on hold, so I can ingrain these routines into my brain, feet, and hands. If there is one thing I am certain of on this vacation, it is that I will leave it a dancer.

"I suck," I admit, sitting on the stage, rubbing my blister-covered heels. We've been practicing for three hours and I'm no better than I was when I got here this morning. I think I may have actually gotten worse, if that's humanly possible.

"You aren't that bad. Most of us have been practicing for days," Autumn says, not meeting my eyes.

"It's okay. I know I suck," I tell her, laughing.

"Okay, so you aren't the most coordinated person I've ever met." She giggles.

"If I have to do jazz hands anymore today, I'm going to get carpal tunnel," I complain, cracking my knuckles. Obviously my hand pain isn't apparent to Catrina, who hands me an orange to peel for her. Somehow, the gloved one has adopted me as her woman servant. Any time she needs something peeled, buttoned, or popped, she comes over to bug me. I peel the orange, break up the sections, and place them on the napkin that Catrina is delicately balancing in her gloved hands. I have to fight the overwhelming urge to rip her gloves off to see what is really underneath. I bet she just has really gross man hands and is too embarrassed to show them! Catrina giggles and rushes off. I shake my head in frustration at Autumn.

Autumn laughs easily while checking her eyeliner for smudges in a compact. Not that she needs to bother because she looks gorgeous even after she's worked up a sweat.

"A few of us are going to the spa later and I was wondering if you would like to join us?" she asks, delicately wiping a few beads of sweat from her brow.

Now normally you would have to pry me kicking and screaming away from a spa. But that's just the cheesy one we have inside the Comfort mall, not the first-class places they have here in Vegas. I mentally calculate how much cash I have left, which takes about two seconds.

"Everything is comped courtesy of the pageant sponsors," she adds.

"Sweet! I'm totally in." Yeah, my first beauty pageant

perk. I wonder if there will be gift bags like at the Oscars?

This will be the perfect opportunity to get the girls to open up and find out if they know anything about Emerson.

I hear a ruckus coming from the other side of the stage. Autumn and I both look over to see the big-haired blonde that tried to bust my chops earlier acting like a drunk person. Autumn covers her mouth with her hand in an attempt to ward off her hysterical laughter.

"I'm really sorry," she says, gulping in some air to try and stop laughing.

"What? I don't get it," I say, as it dawns on me that Big Hair is making fun of me. "Oh, that's hilarious," I yell over to her as she starts an encore because her blond entourage is screaming with laughter.

"Do you have a hair clip?" I ask Autumn, who gives me a confused look but pulls a hair clip out of her makeup bag. I pull out the elastic holding my hair in a ponytail, wrap my hair in a pile on top of my head, and then secure it with the hair clip.

"I don't think you want to provoke her," Autumn says through muffled giggles.

"It takes a lot more than a psycho beauty queen to scare me off," I tell her, while stripping my socks off and stuffing them into my sports bra. "Lipstick," I order, holding my hand out like a surgeon waiting for the proper instrument. Autumn gingerly lays a tube of hot pink lipstick in my palm and I proceed to draw a perfect circle around my lips with it. I check my reflection, which looks completely ridiculous, then strut to the middle of the stage.

"Look, everybody, who am I?" I say, prancing around the stage on my tippy toes.

"You bitch," Big Hair screams, dropping her act and heading straight for me.

She points her hair toward me and comes charging like a deranged bull with a bad hairpiece. The other contestants are riveted and eager for blood, or at least some pulled-out hair and broken nails. At the last second I swing to the left and Big Hair goes steaming by me. I hear a crash and a moan as she plows headfirst into a giant plastic foam Elvis head that we were supposed to dance around as part of the first routine.

"The King is officially dead," I tell Autumn, strutting back over to her. Big Hair is lying dazed in a pile of plastic pieces, rubbing her forehead.

"What the hell is going on in here?" Pageant Mistress screams, coming around the corner of the huge curtain separating the stage from backstage. Great. I have a feeling my pageant days are numbered. I wonder if I can solve the mystery without being a contestant? I quickly unstuff my sports bra, wipe the lipstick off my face, and release the hair clip. Not like it's going to matter because Big Hair is totally going to bust me out anyway. When her evil mother finds out I'm responsible for killing Elvis, I'll be banished from the Miss Teen Queen Pageant forever.

"I got dizzy and I fell into Elvis. I'm really sorry, Mom. I mean, Pageant Mistress."

"Jesus, Mary, and Joseph, Lacy. Can't you do anything right?" she spouts hatefully at her daughter. I have to fight the urge to bolt across the stage, jump on the mistress's back, and get her in a chokehold. If my mom ever talked to me like that, I'd be emancipated in a heartbeat. I hate it, but I actually feel kind of sorry for Big Hair. I mean, Lacy.

⊚

I meet Autumn, Miss Rhode Island, Miss Vermont, and another contestant (who I can't quite place). I decided it wasn't worth troubling my brain to try to learn all forty-nine girls' names. I can usually guess what state they are from by a trait or characteristic anyway. That's how I recognized Miss Vermont, because she smells like maple syrup and always wears UGGs, even for rehearsal.

It's nine o'clock in the morning and we don't have to be back for rehearsals until one this afternoon. Rand is going to take Angel shopping to get her mind off the breakup. My boy is such a sweetie. I've got four hours to bond with these girls and hopefully get some clues about Emerson.

We are giddy and giggling as we push through the

golden doors of the spa to the reception area. Everything is either white or made of glass besides the enormous wall of cascading water behind the desk in the center of the room. A tiny woman dressed in white scrubs with jet-black hair smiles at us then puts her index finger to her lips.

"Welcome to Nirvana," she whispers. "This is our menu for the soul. Take a minute to browse through it and decide what to pamper yourself with," she says softly.

I have to stifle a laugh at her hushed tones. I'm all about tranquility but she's kind of taking it to an unhealthy level.

We all take a copy of the crisp white parchment she is holding out, then form an alliance on the white leather couch. Afraid of being scolded for normal indoor voices, we whisper to each other. We agree that since there are five of us, and since everything is free, we'll have five treatments. We pick the cranberry manicure, the algae wrap, a chocolate facial, the Dead Sea salt glow, and my pick, the hot stone massage.

We quietly return our soul menus and Autumn points to our choices. The receptionist nods in agreement and leads us down a long, narrow hallway. She halts at the end and gestures to the door on the right.

"Hello, ladies. I'm Gert. I'll be your spa technician," a boisterous voice booms, startling the five of us. We file into the room, which contains several large massage tables. Gert instructs us to strip down to our panties and get on top of a table. Each table contains a sheet we can use to cover ourselves once we lie down.

We all get busy peeling off our rehearsal clothes and wrapping ourselves in the sheets, with the exception of the girl I can't place, who strips down to her birthday suit.

"What?" she asks innocently, noticing our stares. "This is just what we do where I'm from," she explains. That's when I remember that she's Miss Missouri, the Show Me state.

We climb onto our tables as delicately as possible and wait for Gert to come back.

"I'm definitely the skinniest girl in this room," Miss Rhode Island says fiercely. I'm about to ask her what the heck that has to do with the price of tea in China when I remember Autumn warning me how sensitive she is about her weight. I sure don't want to be the one who pushes her to purge or anything, so I keep my comment to myself. The other girls must be used to her comments because they just chat amongst themselves like she never even said anything. It would totally suck to have a distorted body image. I'm so lucky. I've always known I look great.

Gert returns with four other spa technicians. After lowering the lights, lighting a few aromatherapy candles, and turning on a CD that sounds like waves crashing against the shore, they begin expertly wrapping each part of our bodies with these white bandages for the algae wrap. I try not to freak out once I realize that I can't move my arms. It's all in the name of beauty, I think, trying to keep my claustrophobia at bay. After smearing my bandages with a dark green paste, she wraps me in a few layers of plastic wrap. I feel like a leftover California roll.

My spa technician starts wiping something that could double as baby poop all over my face. I can smell the chocolate as she massages it into my skin. Okay, I could so live like this.

"This is heaven," I say, hoping to get the girls talking a bit.

"You. No. Talk." Autumn's Asian technician hushes me.

It seems that Gert is the only one who doesn't have serious issues about verbal communication and she's too busy trying to convince Miss Missouri that she would be a perfect candidate for a Brazilian to speak up in my defense. I guess I'll have to find time during one of the other treatments to get the other girls talking about Emerson. I hear a slurping noise to my left and turn my head to see what it is.

Miss Rhode Island is circling her tongue around her mouth and outlying facial area as far as she can reach to lick off her chocolate facial. I start laughing so hard I nearly bust my plastic wrap.

"That's got a ton of calories," I volunteer, unable to resist.

Her eyes, circled in chocolate, bulge out in horror that she hadn't thought of that.

"Get me out of here," she screams at her tech.

Something tells me it's purge time. I feel a tiny bit guilty when I see her flopping around on her table like an epileptic, but it passes when she finally gets upright and hops out of the room like a runaway leftover.

The four of us and our techs howl with laughter, ignoring the SILENCE IS BLISS sign posted on the wall.

Once we finally settle down, no Miss Rhode Island in sight, we each go into our own shower stall and rinse the algae and chocolate off under a raindrop shower. Our techs have left plush robes that feel like they are made of clouds for us to wrap ourselves in.

We return to the first room and climb back on to our respective tables. Soon after, I feel my robe lowered to my waist and hot stones being placed strategically on my back. The only thing that could make this moment any better is if Rand was lying next to me holding my hand. There is no doubt about it. This pageant stuff is hard work.

○

"Aspen, wake up," Autumn says, shaking my arm.

"Huh?" For a second I can't remember where I am but then I feel the cool vinyl of the massage table underneath my bare skin and the dreamy robe tucked around me.

"You've been asleep for three hours," she tells me. I

realize that she is standing next to the table already dressed in her rehearsal clothes. Crap! I slept the whole time? So much for bonding over mani/pedis, I think, wiping drool off my chin.

"If we hurry, we can grab a bite to eat before rehearsal," Autumn says before leaving the room to give me some privacy.

I peel my way-too-relaxed body off the massage table and throw on my clothes, trying to block out the fact that I still have to rehearse more today.

☙

"I can't believe she didn't tell Pageant Mistress on me," I say, before biting into a chicken taco. I'm hoping this conversation will be a bit more productive than the last one, or lack of one, at the spa.

"Lacy really isn't that bad," Autumn says, wiping the corners of her heart-shaped mouth with her napkin. "I'm not trying to stick up for her or anything, but her mom is super hard on her. I'm pretty sure she'll disown her if she doesn't win Miss Teen Queen."

"It's a classic case of projection," I say, happy to be putting my Intro to Psych knowledge to good use.

"Absolutely. Pageant Mistress was first runner-up for Miss Teen Queen in 1989. I think she has serious issues about not winning that tiara," Autumn says.

I try not to choke on my chicken while digesting this new tidbit. All this time I just thought Pageant Mistress was a pageant mom gone rabid. But this new knowledge about her pageant loss takes her behavior to a heightened level of crazy.

But is Pageant Mistress crazy enough over her one-time loss to kidnap a girl she saw as a threat to her daughter winning the pageant? It looks like it is up to me, Miss Illinois, to find out.

☉

I'm totally getting these routines down. Nobody is even laughing at me anymore. Pageant Mistress has stopped giving me death looks and I don't think I've stepped on Autumn's foot more than once this afternoon.

"Okay, you're all dismissed. Be back tonight at ten o'clock for interview rehearsal," Pageant Mistress barks. Most of the girls rush backstage to get into normal clothes to enjoy the rest of their afternoon. I wave good-bye to Autumn and slowly approach Pageant Mistress.

"What do you want, Brooks?"

"I just wanted to let you know that I really appreciate how patient you've been with me while I learn the routines," I lie through my teeth.

"You still suck. I'm moving you to the back row," she says, her back toward me. I have to fight the urge not to knock her clipboard out of her hand and beat her over the head with it. I'm going to be stuck in the back row? Rand won't even be able to see me perform, which was the only highlight of this crappy investigation.

"I'll try harder, Pageant Mistress," I say, knowing that she favors submission in her subordinates. I turn to go and hear the squeak of her shoe turning toward me at the same time.

"What do you really want?" she demands.

"Um, well, somebody told me that you were the first runner-up for Miss Teen Queen and I just thought it would be cool to hear about it," I say, turning back to face her. As I suspected, her face lights up and she has to fight to keep her emotions in check. She pulls something from under the papers on her clipboard and hands it to me. It is a picture of the 1989 Miss Teen Queen and the runners-up. The chestnut-haired queen beams proudly under her tiara with dozens of roses stacked in her arms. My eyes scroll to the right and fall on the scowling face of the first runner-up, a young Pageant Mistress. She is gazing up at the queen with a look of hatred while clutching her single rose so hard that some of the petals are floating to the ground. Yikes, bitter much? I force a smile and hand her back the picture.

"You totally should have won," I add, which melts through a bit of her frosty exterior.

"I know. I had more talent, more brains, and obviously was better looking. But the bitch slept with a judge so she got the tiara."

"That's horrible," I shriek, clutching my chest in fake outrage. "You were totally robbed. I bet you want Lacy to win Miss Teen Queen more than anything in the world," I say, baiting her.

A creepy smile spreads over her prematurely age spot–peppered face and her eyes glaze over a bit. I have to fight the urge to shiver and to ask her why she didn't use a moisturizer with SPF all these years. I don't know that I've ever been stared in the face by such true evil, which is saying quite a bit after dealing with Lulu and Charm. Then just as quickly as her face turned creepy, it turns back, as if she reined in her evil personality—right before my eyes.

"It would be great for me to win. Oops, I mean, Lacy to win, but I'd never do anything to interfere with the sanctity of the judging process," she says, directing her attention back to her clipboard.

"Right. Okay, well, I'll see you tonight," I say, scurrying offstage, confident that I have my first official suspect.

Six

"Omigosh, Rand, this place is amazing!" I exclaim, barely even caring that the heels I borrowed from Angel are digging into the new blisters I got from rehearsal today. Luckily, I was able to browse Angel's travel wardrobe and find a suitable black wraparound dress. I topped it off with some adorable costume jewelry I found in the hotel gift shop, and voilà: I look like a million bucks. That being said, I am still furious about my luggage being lost. The thought of someone pawing through my and Victoria's Secrets gives me the creeps.

"I wanted it to be really special," Rand says, practically blushing. I swear, my boyfriend is the cutest man alive!

"It really is amazing," I reply, forcing my thoughts away from freaks modeling my unmentionables to the romantic candlelit table in the middle of a rain forest. Rand pulls my chair out and I slide delicately into it. I gaze in wonder at the waterfall we are seated directly next to.

"This is so nice," Rand says, melting into his chair.

"I know. This has got to be the coolest restaurant ever," I exclaim, glancing at the leafy canopy above our heads.

"I meant being alone with you," Rand says sweetly.

"Oh, that. Yeah, I suppose the company is pretty good too." I laugh, reaching over to squeeze his hand. Rand always looks handsome but tonight I can tell he made a special effort. He is wearing black Born dress shoes, black slacks, and a tailored ice-blue button-down that hugs his physique. I reach for my napkin to drape in my lap while forcing unladylike thoughts away.

"You look smokin'," he says, reading my mind.

"Behave. You know I have to be back at rehearsal at ten," I remind him. His playful grin slips a bit at the reminder and I want to kick myself for bringing it up. Rand is putting up with Angel crying on his shoulder, me disappearing for most of the day, and who knows what Lucas is dishing out.

"Angel thinks she found you a dress," he says, gazing into the waterfall.

"Let's not talk about the pageant. How is Angel doing anyway?"

"She did okay until she saw Michelangelo's replica of David at Caesars Palace. She started sobbing because it reminded her of Lucas." He grins.

I practically spit my sip of ice water all over him.

"I'm sure they'll work it out when we get back home," Rand says, giving me a chance to catch my breath. "They really are perfect for each other. And who knows? Maybe Angel's right. When you fall in love with someone and you just know that you want to spend the rest of your life with them, why shouldn't the rest of your life start right now?" Rand says passionately.

"Oh, great. Now I'm going to have to deprogram you. You know as well as I do that Angel talks a bunch of smack most of the time." I laugh.

"It makes sense to me though. Why wait? Unless you are waiting for something better to come along," he says tensely. I glance up, suddenly realizing that our conversation has somehow switched from talking about Lucas and Angel's relationship to ours.

"Is that what you think? That I'm waiting for something better to come along?" I practically shriek in anger.

"I'd be a liar if I said it hadn't crossed my mind," he says, stunning me into silence. The waiter comes and we give him our drink order. I pick up my menu, not quite sure how to respond to Rand.

It isn't exactly breaking news that my boy has issues about losing me. He went from being the biggest geek in school to being handpicked by the most prestigious fraternity on campus in under a year. He struggles with his newfound popularity and a part of him still sees me as the unattainable prom queen. But what hurts me most is that I thought Rand knew, with all his heart, how true my love for him is. The thought of being with another boy makes me want to hurl.

"I'm not hungry anymore," I say, putting my menu down.

"I'm sorry, Aspen. I know I'm being irrational, but I just can't help myself from wondering why we are waiting," he says, his voice pleading with me.

"Because we are only nineteen years old. We have no money of our own, no college degrees, no house, nothing. There is a certain order in which things are done. College, job, marriage, and then kids. That's just how normal people do it, Rand." I try not to meet his eyes, knowing that I'm crushing him.

"You're right, I'm sorry. I guess maybe Angel did rub off on me a little bit." He hangs his head.

I reach over our place settings and grab his hand. He looks up at me and in that instant I wish I could make all of his insecurities disappear.

"I know that someday there is nothing that would make me happier than being your wife. And I don't want to wait because I think I'll find somebody better. There is nobody better," I emphasize, squeezing his hand. His mouth pulls up at the corners for the first time in several minutes.

Rand pulls his hand away and covers his face with his palms. "I'm so embarrassed," he says, his voice muffled through his hands.

"Believe me, I get it. You've been under the influence of Angel. Lesser men would have caved by now." I laugh.

"But I'm coming off as this insecure loser boyfriend who wants to do anything to keep other guys away from his girlfriend. It's so alpha male pathetic." He laughs.

"At least you realize that you are alpha male material. That's a start. I know that you know how much I love you. A two-carat diamond isn't going to change that." I wink.

"Two carats, huh? At least I have time to save up." He laughs.

The waiter takes our order, prime rib for Rand, and free-range chicken for me. We table all pageant/marriage talk and spend the rest of the evening admiring each other and sampling each other's dinner. After a scrumptious dessert of cheesecake with raspberry sauce (some of the pageant girls would absolutely freak if they knew how many calories I consumed tonight!) we take the elevator back down to the casino area. I see Rand begin to drool as he spots a Mustang that a lucky slot player can win.

"Why can't I be twenty-one?" he whines, jingling coins in his pocket. I spot a boutique with designer purses and can almost feel myself being drawn to it.

"How about you go this way and I'll go that way?" I point toward the boutique.

"Deal. I'll come find you in twenty." He laughs, bending down for a kiss before we part ways.

I make a beeline for the adorable pink-and-white awning of the store but something catches my eye about halfway there. It is a huge memorial erected in the middle of the lobby. A giant photo in an elaborate gold frame flanks the center of the wall. Gold lettering below the photo spells out the name JESSIE LYNN, with the years 1965–2007 next to it. I look back to the photo. The fortyish-looking woman is lounging on a beach chair with one of those skinny cigarettes dangling from her hot pink lips. Her bouffant brown hair is stuffed on top of her head. And even though she looks like a piece of beef jerky from too much tanning, I can still see a glimmer of the pretty girl she used to be. For a second, I think she looks familiar but then I realize that can't be. Huge candelabras hang alongside the picture and obnoxiously potent flower arrangements, which look eerily like funeral sprays, are standing at attention near the bottom of the memorial. Between the tanning and the ciggies, Jessie's death isn't a real mystery, but I can't help wondering why she is important enough to be memorialized in the Illusions hotel.

"She's a vision," a voice says from behind me. I spin around to see who is checking me out.

"I'm taken, like way taken," I tell the middle-aged man in the tacky leisure suit. I have to bite my tongue not to tell him that I'm not into being some old man's nurse-maid even if I wasn't taken. Then I remember this is the same creep who started talking to me at Pirate's Cove the other day. He must be trolling all the hotels for underaged hotties. He starts laughing and I'm starting to get seriously offended when he extends his hand.

"I was talking about the woman in the photograph," he explains, still holding his hand out. I reach out and shake it quickly. "I'm Cleve Lynn, and that was my wife, Jessie," he says, glancing up at her picture.

"Oh, I'm really sorry," I apologize, feeling ridiculous. "Yes, she was quite the vision." It's not really a lie. She was a vision, just not a pleasant one.

"Are you enjoying your stay at Illusions?" he asks, suddenly turning all concierge on me.

"Oh, I'm not staying here," I say, not divulging any more details. This guy could be a total stalker.

"Right, I knew I recognized you. You took Emerson Chambers's spot in the Miss Teen Queen Pageant," he says, putting a hand on my shoulder. Stalker city. I start to back away slowly when I bump into Rand. He squeezes my arms reassuringly and, just like that, my world is safe again.

"Making new friends without me, Aspen?" Rand asks politely, with just a hint of edge in his voice.

"Hello, son. I'm Cleve Lynn. I'm just making sure that our Miss Teen Queen contestant is having a nice stay," he says, extending his hand to Rand. Rand moves around me and shakes it heartily, without a trace of hostility.

"Of course, Mr. Lynn. All of your hotels are amazing. I'm Rand Bachrach, and this is my girlfriend, Aspen Brooks. We just ate at Amazon and it was a once-in-a-lifetime meal," Rand says, totally kissing his ass. What is going on here?

"I never get tired of hearing that," Mr. Lynn says, slapping Rand on the back so hard he practically falls over.

"I really enjoyed the feature they did on you in *Newsweek* last month. Very inspirational," Rand babbles like a fan girl at a boy band concert. So the guy owns a few hotels in Vegas. Big freaking deal.

"It's mighty good of you to say so, son. I've been pretty blessed," Mr. Lynn says, his eyes stealing another glance at the picture of his deceased wife.

"Aspen, Mr. Lynn is sponsoring the Miss Teen Queen Pageant," Rand explains. I nod my head impressively, wondering how in the world my boyfriend knows this. He must have way too much time on his hands. Then I realize that Cleve Lynn is the one who comped our spa visit. Maybe he isn't so creepy after all.

"I know what it's like to be young and in love so I won't keep the two of you. Good luck with the pageant, Aspen," he says, waving good-bye and disappearing into the casino.

"Holy shit! Do you know who that was?" Rand squeals.

"I'm just going to take a wild guess and say Cleve Lynn," I smart off.

"Aspen, he's one of the richest men in America. He owns practically every hotel on the Strip," he says, nearly hyperventilating. I paste on a fake smile for him, trying to act impressed. Hoover Dam and Vegas businessmen.

These are the things that excite my boyfriend. It is so true that opposites attract.

"You are so crushing on him." I giggle. There is nothing cuter than a boy with a man crush.

"Just think, that could be me someday. Of course, I'd be in the chocolate business, and not the hotel business, but I would still rule," he says dreamily.

"Just promise me something," I beg, weaving my arm through his to steer him back to Pirate's Cove.

"Anything for you, my love," he says, bending down to kiss me.

"Promise me that you will never be caught dead in a polyester leisure suit."

"But I'd look so good doing the John Travolta thing," he teases, working his hips and pointing one arm down and one arm up. I grab his arms and put them back down to his sides before someone escorts him from the hotel.

"It just proves my theory that no amount of money can buy you style." As soon as the words are out of my mouth I realize that I do have a talent for the competition. My sense of style is wicked. I am so going to win this pageant.

○

"Let me make sure I understand this: You want to bring a mannequin onstage and dress it up in different outfits and accessories for your talent?" Pageant Mistress asks, while rubbing her temples vigorously.

"Yeah," I answer.

"Absolutely not. A talent is singing, or dancing, not playing dress-up with an oversized Barbie."

I try hard not to stomp my foot on the stage and roll my eyes. I should have seen this coming. Of course she's not going to let me get up onstage and dazzle the judges with my fashion talent because then Lacy's tap routine will look ridiculous.

"Think of something else," Pageant Mistress says, storming off. I walk back over to stand in line with Autumn and the other girls.

"No go?" Autumn asks, fanning herself with the note card holding her interview question.

"Some people just don't get that looking good is a talent. Sometimes a job. Great, what am I going to do now?" I wonder out loud.

"What are you known for back home?" Autumn asks.

I roll my head around, cracking my neck, while I consider her question. People in Comfort know me as a wronged homecoming queen robbed of her tiara, a prom queen, a beauty, a brain, Rand's girlfriend, Dan and Judy's daughter, a kick-butt girl detective, bff to Tobi, a fun-loving Beta girl, a genius with a few basic Clinique products. The list is endless.

"Thanks, Autumn. You just gave me the most excellent plan," I say, all giddy.

"Uh, my pleasure, I guess." She laughs.

A screeching sound thunders through the auditorium making all of us hold our ears. Pageant Mistress is warming up her bullhorn to start quizzing us on practice interview questions. "Okay, listen up, girls. Things are going to get a lot tougher out there the night of the pageant. I don't want you looking like a bunch of Miss South Carolina 2007s up there. So focus and answer as intelligently as you can.

"Okay, first question. Miss North Dakota. How do you feel about the use of bovine growth hormone in cows to increase production?" Pageant Mistress asks through her staticky bullhorn.

Miss North Dakota teeters on her six-inch heels to the microphone, brushes her platinum bangs out of her eyes, and giggles. "Um, what is, got milk for two hundred?"

I drop my head into my hands and groan as the rest of the girls nearly collapse with laughter. This is going to be the longest night of my life.

❧

I sneak into my hotel room, careful not to let the door slam. Angel is crashed, her mouth hanging open, and a tiny snore escaping. Mona is, of course, sprawled out all over my bed. I undress and slip into one of Angel's T-shirts and attempt to slide into bed. I delicately poke Mona, trying to get her to scoot over but she doesn't move. I'm exhausted and I just want to sleep so I eventually just try shoving her. She's deadweight and doesn't move an inch. Exasperated, I yank the bedspread off of her and curl up on the floor. I have got to find Emerson so that she and Mona are reunited and I can get my bed back.

I feel like I have just shut my eyes when the alarm goes off. Angel grunts then slams her hand down on top of it to stop the offending noise. I stretch out, expecting my entire body to scream with pain from rehearsal and sleeping on the floor, but am surprised to find that I don't feel that bad at all. Then I realize that I'm not on the floor. I'm in my bed. And Mona is nowhere to be found. I guess I must have crawled up here in my sleep or something. Weird.

"If it isn't Little Miss Teen Queen," Angel smarts off, rolling over to face me.

"Don't start giving me a bunch of crap. I don't like missing out on my vacation either, but somebody had to step up and look for Emerson." I roll out of bed and start going through Angel's clothes for some clean underwear.

"Don't even think about it," Angel says, eyeing the green thong in my hand.

"Believe me, I'm tempted to just go caveman, but that is just too gross."

"Look in that bag over there," she says, gesturing to a hot pink bag on top of the armoire. I pull it down and nearly squeal over the contents. Several pairs of silky briefs with tags on them smile back at me.

"You bought me underwear!" I shout, running to the bed to hug her.

"I guess this makes it official. We are truly friends." She laughs, hugging me back. "And did Rand tell you about that gown I found?"

"He mentioned something, but you know guys, I didn't even bother asking him to describe it or I would have been picturing something from Goodwill. Maybe we can go tonight after rehearsal and I can try it on." I head for the bathroom to take a quick shower, feeling guilty when I see Angel's smile disappear. I know that she is wishing she were spending the day with Lucas.

"Why don't you just make up already?" I ask her, peeking my head out of the bathroom.

"I don't know," she says sadly. I sneak a peek at the clock and realize that as much as I would love to spend the morning analyzing Angel's irrational thought processes on teenage marriage, I've got to get to rehearsal. I jump in the shower, mentally promising to make it up to her later with a shopping trip and a visit to the Cheesecake Factory.

◎

I find Mona at a table downstairs in the lobby near the complimentary breakfast table. She is staring into a cup of coffee so intently that I am nervous to interrupt her for fear of getting hot coffee thrown on me. I grab a miniature box of Froot Loops and make a big production about opening the box and crunching on a few very loudly. She finally looks up at me and slowly the look of complete helplessness fades to a fake smile.

"Good morning, Mona. Sorry if I squashed you this morning when I got into bed," I say with a laugh, hoping to lighten her mood.

"Oh, you didn't. I picked you up and put you in bed when I got up. You just looked so uncomfortable on the floor." She lifts her coffee and takes a cautious sip.

"You picked me up and put me in bed?" I ask, stunned. I'm not sure if I should be touched or creeped out by this gesture.

"Sweetie, don't let the press-ons fool ya," she says, holding up her hands. "I've been helping my husband run a dairy farm for the last twenty years. Shoveling cow manure is a great workout." She laughs.

I nearly gag on my Froot Loops. I resist the urge to thank Mona for the visual of a steaming pile of cow crap but only because I feel sorry for her. She's broke and alone in a strange city. With her only daughter missing. And those fake nails are just tragic.

"I think I've got a suspect," I tell her.

"Oh my goodness," she says very slowly. "Tell me everything."

"I don't want to point any French-manicured fingers just quite yet," I tell her, afraid that she might make a spectacle and scare off my suspect.

"Aspen, I'm going crazy just hanging around this hotel all day," she says, getting flustered. "Please tell me what I can do to help you."

She looks so desperate, and it's not just the generic makeup. I know she is terrified that something really bad may have happened to Emerson.

"Um, well. I'm just going to say that I think Emerson is fine and I have a feeling that once the pageant is over she will turn up."

"I hope your hunch is right. So can I tag along with you?"

It would be really rude to tell a distraught mother that I just don't do partners. It just never works out. Harry is the closest I've ever come to having a partner and that's just because he's allowed to carry a gun. I've got to think up some mindless task for Mona to do today.

As luck would have it, Cleve Lynn strolls right through the lobby dressed as if he is color-blind.

"See that dude in the hideous golf pants?" I ask Mona.

She nods, tracking Cleve with her overshadowed eyes.

"He owns this hotel. Try to persuade him to show you the surveillance tapes from the night that Emerson disappeared."

Mona bolts out of her chair like a rocket and steams

toward Cleve. I already know that a mogul like Cleve Lynn isn't going to let Mona anywhere near his precious surveillance tapes without a search warrant, but at least it will keep her busy for a while.

Seven

"I've got a suspect," I whisper into the phone, while hiding in the same lobby alcove where I overheard Emerson's phone call the night she went missing.

"Who is this?" Detective Grant asks. I can almost hear her snarl through the phone.

"This is Aspen Brooks. I'm working the missing pageant contestant case," I tell her through clenched teeth. It's like she doesn't even care that a girl is out there alone somewhere.

I hear a loud noise like the phone got dropped followed by several minutes of hysterical laughter. I tap my foot on the marble floor while silently cursing the detective for wasting my precious cell phone minutes. She'd better pray that I'm not roaming. Catrina walks up and hands me her can of soda. I pop the top and hand it back to her. She happily goes on her way. It's always something with that girl. I don't even think she wipes herself with those precious hands.

"Um, I wasn't aware that we had put you on the Force," Detective Grant says when she finally decides to pick the phone back up.

"Well somebody has to do your job while you are busy sitting around eating doughnuts," I smart off.

"Listen here, you snotty little . . ."

"I wouldn't finish that if I were you. Do you want my information or should I continue investigating this case by myself?" I can't believe the attitude on this chick. If she weren't so hideous looking, I'd actually think she was a diva, but I'm pretty sure there is some kind of looks prerequisite to be a diva.

"Okay, Miss Brooks, who's your big suspect?" she asks in a condescending tone.

"It's the woman in charge of the beauty pageant. She's behind the whole thing. I think she kidnapped Emerson to get her out of the pageant so her daughter could win," I say quickly.

"Hmm . . . so you think that a grown woman would risk going to jail just so that her daughter could win a beauty pageant?" she asks with a smirk that I can definitely hear.

"You don't get it. She's got all these residual issues

from this pageant that she lost. Winning is all about her, not her daughter."

"Residual issues about losing a beauty pageant, huh?"

"I know you think I'm just some teenager who doesn't know anything, but I can spot somebody with issues a mile away. I've dealt with psycho ex-beauty queens [Lulu] and hardcore perfectionists [Charm], so I know what I'm looking at here. She makes us call her Pageant Mistress. for God's sake," I say, hating that I'm sort of pleading with her to take me seriously.

"Okay, okay. I know you've got good instincts; at least that is what Detective Malone vouched for. I'll check out this Pageant Mistress. Any clue on her real name?" she asks, making some background noise that sounds like looking for a pen. Crap. I didn't even think to get Pageant Mistress's last name.

"Her first name is Andrea and she was the first runner-up in the 1989 Miss Teen Queen Pageant. Oh, and she has a daughter named Lacy who has really big hair."

I hear a sound almost like a small gasp. Even I am embarrassed about my lack of attention to detail on this one. It's just that I want to be lying out at the pool so much more than I want to be prancing around like a show dog onstage. I've got to get my edge back and find out everything I can about Pageant Mistress.

"I realize that this isn't a whole lot of information to go on but I'll get you more as soon as I can. Maybe if you can just come down to talk to her, poke around a little bit . . ." I say, nervous that the detective hasn't responded yet. If she doesn't start taking this seriously, I swear, I'm going to freak out.

"Are you sure it was the 1989 Miss Teen Queen Pageant?" Detective Grant asks.

"I'm positive. She even showed me the picture of her with the winner. She sure hated that girl. She said she cheated and slept with a judge. How foul is that?"

"Listen, I've got a pretty heavy caseload but I'll try to do some snooping around," she says, then hangs up on me. I hold my phone out, stunned. Her phone etiquette is almost as bad as her split ends.

☉

"I've got the whole day off. Where do you want to do me? I mean, what do you want to do?" I giggle into my phone. Pageant Mistress wanted some time to sightsee with Lacy so she gave us the rest of the day off. She isn't fooling me though; she'll be working Lacy like a twelve-year-old in a Chinese sweatshop, but I don't care because I'm ready for some R & R with Rand.

"That's awesome. And I have a surprise for you too. Why don't you come to my room?" Rand asks ecstatically.

"I'll be there in five," I say, hanging up. I check my

reflection in the mirror then glance over to the note Mona taped to it. Cleve wouldn't agree to let her see the tapes. Not a big surprise there. I'll have to work on Detective Grant about that. Mona's note also says that she made missing posters and is off plastering the city. Surely our combined efforts will turn up some clues soon. I head off to Rand's room only to run into the Dakota twins on the elevator.

"Hi, we've never actually met. I'm Aspen," I say, extending my hand toward the brunette.

"I'm Miss South Dakota," she says, giving me a grin that is nearly blinding. She ignores my hand like she doesn't understand what I'm doing. I direct it at the blonde, thinking she'll know that she is supposed to shake back. She stands there looking confused, blowing a huge bubble that pops, splattering gum over her mouth and nose.

"I'm Miss North Dakota," she says, after retrieving all her gum off her face with a tongue so long she could rival Gene Simmons. I'm so not hungry after witnessing that.

"What are your real names?" I ask, retracting my hand.

They look at each other and start giggling. I glance in the mirror-covered wall of the elevator to make sure something horrible didn't happen to my face in the last five minutes. Nope, I still look gorgeous.

"Those are our names, silly," they answer back in unison.

"Right . . ." I respond, bolting off the elevator as soon as the door opens, not even caring if I'm on the right floor.

☙

"What is going on in here?" I ask, rushing past Rand to find Angel practically catatonic, surrounded by room service trays.

"She won't go anywhere. She just sits there eating and watching this hotel channel on how to play blackjack," Rand whispers, looking worried.

So much for my day off.

"Angel, are you okay?" I ask, moving a plate of shrimp cocktail to the side so that I can sit down.

She glances up from red-rimmed eyes and surprise registers on her face. It's like she didn't even hear me come in. I've seen a lot of breakup casualties in my day but Angel looks like she is about a cheeseburger away from becoming completely detached from reality. She doesn't answer me but directs her attention back to learning all about doubling down. Rand sits down on the bed across from us and gives me a look of concern.

"This behavior isn't acceptable, Angel. I have one day off and I don't want to ruin it by babysitting some zoned-out tragedy case. Get up, we're going to the pool," I say in a very harsh tone. She doesn't move or take her eyes from the TV. Rand shrugs like he doesn't know what else to do. He points to one of the uncovered trays. I pick the lid up to find an untouched BLT and french fries. I start chowing down while mentally assessing the Angel situation.

After my third bite, I contemplate just leaving her here. She's nineteen years old and she can take care of herself. She is the one who broke up with Lucas and caused this anyway. But as I'm wolfing down some fries I realize that if I was the one who was boyfriendless on spring break, I wouldn't want to be left alone. Sometimes it is a curse how good of a friend I am. I finish the sandwich and fries while devising a plan.

"Angel, you have one more opportunity to get up and come with us," I warn her. She doesn't take her eyes off the blackjack dealer on the flat screen.

"Okay, you were warned," I say, grabbing her arms. "Rand, grab her legs and help me carry her into the bathroom."

"This is kind of crossing an imaginary boundary that I have for myself," Rand says, hesitant.

"Do you want to spend the day with me or not?" I ask, surprised that Angel isn't flailing around. She is still sitting perfectly still even though I've got a death grip on her arms.

"Okay, okay," Rand finally agrees, grabbing Angel's ankles and helping me maneuver her into the shower. I turn on the cold water full blast but she just stands there like a zombie.

"That's it. I'm having you admitted to the psych ward," I say, almost out the door to dial 911.

"He hasn't stayed here for two nights," Angel yells

suddenly, then collapses in a heap in the bathtub. Rand shuts off the water and wraps a towel around her shoulders, then moves out of the way so I can sit down on the toilet next to her.

"That doesn't mean anything, Angel. He's probably just out walking the Strip all night," I say confidently, hoping that Lucas doesn't revert to his man-whore ways.

"I know he met someone," Angel says, sobbing into her hands.

"Okay, so he might be having a little fling. It's not like anything is going to come of some girl he meets on spring break. They'll never have what you and Lucas have."

Angel starts wailing so loud that I'm afraid hotel security will be called. I start rubbing her back through her soaked T-shirt to try to calm her down.

"How would you feel if Rand was with someone else?" Angel mumbles, causing me to nearly double over in pain at the very thought. Rand and I lock eyes and silently tell each other that would never happen.

"Rand and I will find him for you," I tell Angel. "You get some beauty sleep." God knows she is going to need it, I think, helping a drowned rat–looking Angel out of the tub.

◎

"You look hot," Rand says, winking at me.

"I totally do, don't I?" I say, admiring my bikini-clad

self in the full-length mirror. Rand's surprise was that my suitcase finally got here. To my total amazement all my stuff was inside and appeared untampered with by freaks. At first, I thought there was some mistake because when I opened my suitcase there was an exquisite violet evening gown carefully folded on top. But then I checked the tag to see that it was a Judy Brooks original and knew my mom had snuck it in to surprise me. I swear, my mom is the coolest. The gown will be perfect for the pageant.

"Are you ready for some fun in the sun?" Rand asks me, looking completely adorable in navy blue swim trunks with a towel wrapped around his neck.

"Just remember we have to keep an eye out for Lucas too," I say, feeling slightly guilty that I sent Angel back to our room to take a nap on the pretense that I'd be out scouring Las Vegas for Lucas.

"If I know Lucas, he'll be sunning himself, probably surrounded by thong-wearing beauties." Rand laughs, holding the door open for me.

"You are so right." I sigh, kind of hoping that we don't find him so we can relax.

◎

My claws are officially out. The pool area is filled with pageant contestants and other female spring breakers who are not getting that Rand is totally spoken for. It is driving me crazy how they are mentally undressing him.

This is not going to be so relaxing after all. We are weaving in and out of deck chairs, trying to find a spot.

"I'm about ready to just dump somebody's stuff off. I mean, how rude is it to put your crap there and then take off and not sit there all afternoon," I whine.

"Don't stress, Aspen. Come this way," Rand says, grabbing my hand and guiding me toward a cabana. I notice a sign that reads RESERVED FOR BACHRACH hung on the side of a banana-colored cabana.

"When did you do this?" I squeal.

"I'll never reveal my secrets," Rand says, holding back the flap of the cabana so that I can go in.

"This is the coolest thing ever," I say, taking in the pillow-topped deck chairs, cooler full of pop and juice, and the tiny table filled with snacks. I drag the chairs together and flop down on one. Rand drops our towels and lies down beside me.

"You are the coolest thing ever," he says, stroking my hair. He leans over and starts kissing me and I'm pretty sure this is the closest I'll get to heaven for a while. If I'm going to be honest about when I knew deep down that Rand was the one, I'd have to say it was after the first time he kissed me. I'd never had a kiss reach all the way down into my toes before like Rand's did. It took me some time to admit that we should be together, but eventually I figured it out.

"We are never going to break up," I say, pulling out of the kiss, not sure whether I'm asking him or telling him.

"Never," he promises, looking so far into my eyes it

makes me want to cry. We melt into each other again and I make myself burn the image of this moment into my mind forever.

"I love you, Aspen Brooks," he whispers, moving down to kiss my neck.

"I love you too. Lucas?"

"What the . . ." Rand shouts, thinking I've accidentally called him by the wrong name. As if!

I bolt up, seeing Lucas sneering at us while holding up the flap of the cabana.

"Are you becoming a voyeur now, Lucas, since you aren't getting any?" I yell, angry with him for interrupting such a magical moment.

"Ahoy! The hell you say. I've got girls swarming on me like shark on chum." Lucas laughs, walking in, grabbing a pop, and sitting at the end of my deck chair.

"Stop talking like that. You're not even doing it right. You can't just use one pirate word in a sentence and expect people to take you seriously. That's your problem, Lucas. You're never serious about anything," I yell at him. I can't believe that I'm ruining my spring break trying to find his friend and he's busy chasing girls.

"Aspen, you aren't being fair," Rand says. "Angel is the one who broke up with him."

I'm about to slug Rand for standing up for Lucas until I see Lucas's goofy grin fall at the mere mention of Angel. A faint memory of Lucas standing at my dorm room door comes flooding back to me. It was last year and Lucas was worried sick about Angel because she wasn't returning his calls. He drove all the way up in the middle of the night to find her. That's when I knew that he really loved her. And he still does.

"I haven't been with anyone else. I've just been going around to the clubs in the hotels showing Emerson's picture around to see if anyone recognizes her," he says, pulling one of Mona's crinkled fliers from the pocket of his cargo shorts.

I officially feel like a piece of crap.

"I'm sorry, Lucas. I was out of line. I'm just bummed that this vacation is turning out to be so much work." And it's not like I can totally blame Lucas and Angel. Why do I have to get myself involved in these mysteries? I think my parents let me watch too much *Scooby-Doo* during my formative years.

"Let's just figure out how we are going to get you guys back together, okay?" I say. Lucas nods enthusiastically, and even though he is wearing an eye patch, I know he's all business.

○

I felt like we would all work better if we were drifting down the lazy river ride at our hotel pool. Our tubes are hooked together and we've spent the last two hours floating down the sun-warmed water discussing our strategy, breaking only when the current leads us under the giant waterfall.

"What if she doesn't go for it?" Rand says, a little unsure of the boldness of my plan.

I dip my toe in the water and bring it back up fast to splash him a little, my only response to his ridiculous question.

"I hate to admit it, but Aspen is usually right," Lucas says, shielding his eyes from the sun.

"Just one last thing," I tell them, knowing it is time to get out of the sun before I get sunburnt and can't do my routines. "She can't ever know. She'll feel like we betrayed her. She has to believe that she made this choice on her own."

I feel a little guilty pulling on Angel's puppet strings like I know the plan is going to, but in the end, it's for the greater good. The future of Lucas and Angel, who are just as perfect together as Rand and I. Okay, maybe that's stretching things a bit far, but seriously, who else is ever going to put up with either one of them?

⊚

"She isn't even giving my case the time of day," I tell Rand as we share a table under a giant umbrella at the poolside café.

"In defense of Detective Grant, maybe Emerson did just walk away," Rand says, playing devil's advocate. I hate it when he does that.

"Maybe she's just lazy," I huff, taking another bite of my club sandwich.

"Maybe Emerson didn't want to take responsibility for bailing her family out. Maybe she just wanted to have fun," Rand says, carving off a piece of his prime rib. This is the third time Rand has ordered prime rib since we got to Vegas. He is such a total carnivore.

"There's something about this detective though. I feel like she's normally a real workhorse. I think she has a grudge against beauty pageants. Most ugly people do."

Rand half-snorts, half-laughs at my statement and when I raise my eyebrows at his response he shovels a forkful of creamed spinach into his mouth so he can't get himself into more trouble.

"I'm a little nervous about this plan with Angel," he finally says.

"What? The worst thing that could possibly happen is that they end up married." I laugh, savoring the last bite of my sandwich.

❧

"How about this one?" Lucas says, gesturing to a gigantic cubic zirconia in a sterling silver setting.

"We want her to actually think that it is real, Lucas," I say, fighting not to roll my eyes. Boys are so dense when it comes to the four Cs.

"This is it," I say, handing him a half-carat princess cut in a fourteen-karat-gold setting.

"It's pretty small," he says, handing it back to me. He starts to fondle a fake emerald as big as my head.

"Do you want my help or not?" I say, looking around for Rand. He wandered off to get us some ice cream, completely uninterested in helping shop for Angel's fake engagement ring.

"This just feels kind of mean, like I'm lying to her," Lucas says, running a hand through his shoulder-length blond hair.

"Nobody wants to see Angel get hurt, especially me. But this is what she thinks she wants, so you have to give it to her. I promise you that she is going to see the craziness behind it and will be begging you to wait until you're thirty to get married. We are only doing this to get the two of you back together," I reassure him.

"How much for this?" I ask the uninterested teenaged girl running the costume jewelry kiosk.

"I dunno." She shrugs. "Seven bucks?"

I peel off a five and a couple singles and hand it to her. I hold the ring out to Lucas.

"You do want to marry her someday, don't you?" I ask him as he gingerly takes the ring and slips it into his pocket. He brightens at my question.

"She's my soul mate," he answers confidently.

"Then it's not a lie," I say, putting my arm around his shoulders and leading him off to find Rand.

Eight

"Wear something fancy that doesn't look like a dead animal," I tell Angel as we get ready for dinner.

"I'm not going. You and Rand should be alone," Angel says, not moving from the bed. She ordered another round of room service this afternoon and every time she moves a tiny bit the bed clanks from all the trays banging together.

"We were alone today," I lie. "We really want you there," I plead. This is the biggest part of the plan and if I can't get Angel to dinner the whole plan goes down in flames.

"I just don't feel like going out," she whines.

I slam the bathroom door hoping that she will cave when she thinks I'm mad. I'm nearly finished applying my makeup when she knocks lightly on the door. When I open it, she is standing there, looking pitiful, but dressed in a flame-red cocktail dress.

"Sit down," I say, gesturing to the toilet. "I'll do your hair and makeup."

I can't believe it when she doesn't even fight me. I use my curling iron to flip her ebony locks up on the ends then spray it so it doesn't fall. I use my natural-born makeup skills to turn her from a mess to a marvel. I can hardly believe my eyes when I'm done. Angel looks positively fabulous. I have truly outdone myself.

"I'm done," I announce proudly and gesture toward the mirror for her to look. She turns slowly, then for the first time in days, a genuine grin spreads across her lovely face.

"I can't believe we used to be enemies," she says, with tears in her eyes.

"We just misunderstood each other. Those days are long gone," I reassure her. That's the one thing I never realized about Angel before we were friends: how incredibly insecure she is. She puts one face on for strangers, but only her friends know the truth of just how vulnerable she really is. That's why she keeps making Lucas prove himself. Deep down she's afraid someday he'll just go away for good.

"Friends forever?" she asks, careful to leave off the "best" because she knows I've always classified Tobi as my best friend.

"Best friends forever," I answer back, knowing that my heart is way big enough for more than one best friend.

☙

"You look downright dashing this evening, Mr. Bachrach," I tell my date, squeezing his leg under the table.

"You clean up pretty well yourself, Miss Brooks. Although that bikini you were wearing today holds a special place in my heart." He grins devilishly.

"Did you guys see Lucas at the pool today?" Angel asks, trying to be sly. She immediately covers her face with her menu, afraid of her reaction to our answer.

Rand gently bumps my leg under the table and I look up to see a tuxedo-clad Lucas walking through the restaurant carrying a dozen red roses. People look up from their meals as he walks by, sensing that something amazing is about to happen.

I lock eyes with Lucas and suddenly I think he might puke right into the roses, but he keeps trudging forward toward our table. Angel fidgets in her seat, thinking Rand and I aren't wanting to tell her what we witnessed today. Lucas comes right up behind Angel, takes a deep breath, and then moves to the side so that she can see him.

The next few seconds are like slow motion. Angel drops her menu and lets out a bit of a sigh at the sight of Lucas.

I have to admit that with his slicked-back hair and tuxedo, he is totally sigh-worthy. Lucas hands Angel the flowers then bends on one knee. What were only whispers from fellow diners have turned into oohs and aahs as they realize what is happening. Lucas fidgets in his pocket for a minute, only to extract a ring. I know immediately that this isn't the seven-dollar ring that I picked out. Even from across the table I can tell that the ring Lucas is holding out to Angel is no fake.

"Angelique Martina Ives, will you marry me?" Lucas asks, with trepidation.

I look back to Angel who is sitting with her mouth hanging open. I kick her from under the table to get her to rejoin our planet. She blinks hard, then throws the roses on the table.

"Oh, Lucas, you had me at yo ho," she says, lunging for Lucas, wrapping her arms around his neck.

I groan and throw my face into my hands at Angel's reply. Only these two would get each other enough to speak pirate. Cheers go up from around the restaurant as they assume the hug to mean yes. Rand reaches for my hand, obviously touched by Lucas's gesture. I am too stunned by the round carat solitaire that Lucas is slipping onto Angel's left ring finger to say anything. I've known Lucas Riley longer than I've known Rand or Angel and I know this isn't an act for him. He really wants to marry Angel. Now.

Ⓢ

Dinner was completely gag worthy. Not the food—that was divine—but watching Lucas and Angel paw each other and discuss which wedding chapel to get married at. I should have known that Lucas wouldn't follow through with my plan. The boy cannot be trusted with anything important. Once, when Lucas and I were dating, I gave him my brand-new white Dooney purse to hold while we were at the movies. When I got back from the bathroom he had it sitting on the toxic movie theater floor. I spent half the movie in the bathroom trying to detox my purse. I should have known this situation wouldn't fare any better.

"So, where did you get the money for the ice?" I ask Lucas, gesturing to Angel's sparkling new accessory.

"When I was out asking people if they had seen Emerson, I started stopping at Illusions for free soda. I dropped a couple coins in a slot and won three hundred dollars. I just kept winning. Eventually it added up to a pretty big chunk of change. Dinner's on me tonight, by the way." He laughs. Rand gives him a high five.

"They didn't even card you?" I ask in amazement.

"Nope. I had me some complimentary cervezas too," Lucas boasts proudly. I fight the urge to tell him that he won't even be allowed to drink at his own wedding if he goes through with it.

"That's a nice place your idol is running," I say, bumping Rand's arm. He looks disappointed, but I don't know if it's because Cleve Lynn got knocked off his pedestal or because Rand could have gambled the other night and gotten away with it.

"How's the rehearsal going, Aspen?" Angel asks, while offering Lucas a bite of her steak.

I brighten, hoping this is a chance to turn the discussion from how getting married in the same chapel as Britney Spears is nothing but bad luck to how evil Pageant Mistress is. They won't even remember they are engaged when I get done filling them in.

"You wouldn't believe how incredibly disturbed the lady running the pageant is. I'm talking whacked with a capital W," I say, reeling them in.

"Seriously? Like Lulu whacked or Charm whacked?" Angel inquires with huge, inquisitive eyes.

"Kind of a combo of the two with a double side of God complex. She actually makes us call her Pageant Mistress," I add, cringing.

Angel nearly spits out a drink of her iced tea. Lucas takes his cloth napkin and delicately wipes her mouth for her.

"What night is the pageant?" Lucas asks, cramming another dinner roll into his mouth.

"Tomorrow night," I answer, feeling butterflies in my stomach. I haven't even tried on Emerson's routine costumes yet to make sure they fit. I haven't had the gown

Mom made me pressed. I haven't figured out who I'm going to use as my "before" subject for my makeover talent. I haven't thought up what I'm going to tell Pageant Mistress my talent is since I know she won't approve my makeover talent. And most of all, I haven't figured out what Pageant Mistress did with Emerson. Tears crowd my eyes and threaten to ruin my perfect makeup.

"It'll be fine, Aspen. I can't wait to see you onstage," Rand says, sensing how overwhelmed I am.

"Yeah, Aspen. We're all going to be there," Angel says excitedly.

"So is this thing, like, broadcast to the entire world?" Lucas asks, nearly giving me heart failure. Somehow I had almost forgotten that millions of people would be watching me rock out. What if I'm not as good as I think I am? What if Pageant Mistress is right and I do have two broken left feet? I'm feeling dizzy from the pressure.

Suddenly Rand gestures urgently at our waiter.

"We're going to need a chocolate mousse here, ASAP," Rand tells him, very seriously. The waiter rushes to a dessert cart and back to our table in record time. Rand dips a spoon in the fluffy confection then feeds it to me. I start to feel my normal confidence come flooding back as Rand feeds me more chocolate. I do rock. I'll send my gown to the dry cleaner's tomorrow. And I get a flash of who would be the ultimate candidate for a makeover. I'll think up something totally ridiculous for my talent so that Pageant Mistress doesn't feel threatened. All is right in Aspen world tonight.

"Here's to my soon-to-be bride," Lucas announces, holding up a champagne flute full of Sprite.

Okay, everything except that one teensy thing.

⊙

"That didn't look like an act to me," Rand says, as we stroll along the Miracle Mile shops of the Planet Hollywood hotel. We ditched the engaged ones, as we are now referring to them, on two agreed-upon conditions. Our condition was that they didn't elope without us. And theirs was that we didn't go to Rand's room for at least three hours. Gag!

"Unfortunately, it was as real as the ring," I say, stopping to drool over a killer sundress.

"Are you going to try and stop them?" Rand asks in a strange tone.

"What? You don't think I should?" I ask, stunned, walking away from the dress.

"I just think that sometimes you have to let go. Let people do whatever they are going to do. You can't control every situation, Aspen." Rand walks over to a bench and takes a seat, suddenly looking weary.

"You think I'm controlling?" I demand, following him to the bench.

He runs a hand through his curls, not meeting my eyes.

"You do, don't you?" I demand, jamming my fists on my hips.

He looks up at me with those evergreen eyes that could melt the Grinch's heart and shakes his head.

"I think you would do just about anything to protect the people you love. I just know that you can't always save them from getting hurt. Sometimes you just have to be there to catch them when they fall," he says, pulling me onto his lap.

"Don't you know how hard it is for me to keep watching you deliberately get yourself into dangerous situations? But I don't ever tell you to stop, do I?"

I shake my head, suddenly feeling very guilty about my amateur sleuthing when I see it from Rand's eyes.

"And I never would. Sometimes loving somebody means you have to let them make their own mistakes," he says, brushing a stray hair behind my ear.

"But don't you think it's crazy for them to get married? They are so young," I plead, desperate for him to agree with me.

"Who is to say what is too young to fall in love. My grandparents got married when they were eighteen, and so did my parents. I've never seen two couples more in love, well, except your parents," he says, laughing. My parents, Dan and Judy, are kind of known for their PDAs. They are totally cute.

I contemplate Rand's argument for a minute while I rest my head on his shoulder. I suppose I do have some control tendency issues. I've already got this whole missing pageant girl mystery going on, not to mention the pageant itself. Maybe I should just butt out of the whole Lucas and Angel debacle.

"But I'm kind of responsible for this since it was my idea to fake propose to her," I say, unwilling to let go.

"It would have happened anyway. Let it go, Aspen," Rand says, pulling me close.

Rand is right. I can't be held responsible for the actions of the two most impulsive people on the planet. If they want to get married, I'll just show up as the maid of honor and keep my mouth shut. I relax into Rand's arms feeling better already having ditched one of my catastrophes. That is why Rand is so perfect for me. He balances me out. Sometimes I wonder if he ever gets tired of it.

"I'm sorry you aren't having a very good time," I apologize, realizing for the first time that my actions aren't only dominating my vacation but Rand's too.

"Any time with you is a good time," he assures me, kissing the top of my head. "Besides, I'm just looking forward to seeing you perform and walk onstage in that gown."

"I'm still so nervous that I'll fall," I confess.

"You'll be exquisite," Rand promises.

"Yeah, I guess I should call my parents to tell them

I'm going to be on live television," I say, blowing off the fact that I haven't told Rand that Pageant Mistress has me squirreled away in the back row and he'll be lucky if he can even see my feet.

"I already did it," he assures me.

"What did they say?" I ask, amazed that Rand would think to call them. That's my boyfriend, courteous to a fault.

"Your mom said something about how she is sure you'll be great and how she is sure that knocking your tooth out while practicing ballet could happen to any-one."

I guess that explains the memory I had of the little girl wiping out. Lovely.

"They figured you were up to something but I distracted your mom pretty quick by reminding her that her gown would be seen by millions of people."

"Good save," I tell him, giving him a quick peck. My mom knows me pretty well and knows that it would take a force of nature to get me onstage with a bunch of dim-witted pageant contestants, with the exception of Autumn. "What would I do without you?" I ask Rand, staring dreamily into his eyes.

"I hope you don't ever have to find out," he tells me, sealing it with one of his delicious kisses.

◎

"I came by the hotel but I wasn't able to get to your Pageant Mistress because you were all busy rehearsing. I should be able to swing by tomorrow though," says Detective Grant.

"That's funny because rehearsal was dark today," I say, not sure if I'm more excited to use a cool Las Vegas show term or to bust out the lazy detective.

Nothing but dead air comes across my cell phone for a few seconds. Detective Grant obviously left her poker voice at home since she isn't even bothering to defend herself.

"Can you hear me now?" I ask, cracking myself up.

"The truth is, Aspen, no one has even filed a missing persons report on Emerson Chambers, so my hands are tied. If you want to have her mother come down and fill out a report then I might take another look at the case. But until then, please don't bother me again."

No, she didn't just say that to me. Mona tried to file a report but she told us it was too soon. We just assumed it would get filed when the police realized Emerson never came back. Now she mentions this three days later, what gives? The hair on the back of my neck is standing straight up, which can only mean one thing. The detective is hiding something.

"I really appreciate all your help, Detective. I promise I won't bug you again. There's just one more thing I was wondering about though. I was going through Emerson's things and I found a death threat. I'm sure it's nothing but I just thought . . ."

"Why didn't you call me immediately?" Detective Grant shouts, now fully on the case.

"I didn't want to bother you," I tell her, running my free hand through the cool water of the fountain in front of the Paris hotel.

"I need to see that note immediately," she demands.

"The thing is, I kind of loaned my Dooney out to my friend and the note is inside of it. And she's going to be gone until tomorrow night," I lie, winking at Rand.

"What's a Dooney?"

I suppress a huge sigh about her utter stupidity. She really is worse off than I thought.

"My Dooney & Bourke purse," I tell her in fashion victim layman's terms.

"And you won't get it back until tomorrow night?"

"Yeah, she won't be back with it until right before the pageant starts. Could you meet me backstage at six o'clock and I'll give it to you then?"

"Uh, sure. What exactly did the note say? Did it just threaten Emerson or all of the contestants?"

"It was definitely focused on Emerson," I assure her, knowing how much she would love to shut down the pageant.

"Okay, I'll see you tomorrow then. And, Aspen, no more snooping around," she says, clicking off.

Me? Snoop around? As if!

"Okay, what have you got up your sleeve this time?" Rand asks, knowing that no one on the planet would ever get to borrow any of my Dooneys.

"Just a little surprise for Detective Grant for being so incredibly useless."

"That wasn't true about the death threat, was it?" Rand asks, suddenly worried.

"No. If you want to know the truth, I'm starting to wonder if Emerson did just take off on her own."

"But you aren't sure enough to drop this whole thing. Are you, Nancy Drew?" Rand teases.

"As if. I'm totally better dressed than she ever was," I retort, giving him a little splash from the fountain.

"Oh, you're going to pay for that," Rand says, cupping his hands and filling them with water.

"You wouldn't," I shriek, trying to run from him. I smack into someone at the same moment that a few errant drops of water land on my head. The rest of the water splashes right into the face of the person I nearly tackled.

"I'm so sorry," I say, backing away.

"That's perfectly fine. I've got another one of these tucked away in my closet," Cleve Lynn says, brushing water off his tuxedo.

"Mr. Lynn, I'm so incredibly sorry," Rand says, looking like he is about to burst into tears.

"It's just water, my boy," Cleve assures him, although it looks like he was spiffed up to go somewhere pretty fancy. And he might have another tux at home but the water messed up his Donald Trump hair pretty good too. I consider offering him a scrunchie to pull it back but then reconsider.

"We were just having some fun. Aspen's been really busy with the pageant and we haven't gotten much time together. I just really miss her and I wasn't thinking," Rand mumbles. I put my hand on his arm to hopefully help stop his verbal diarrhea. I can't believe how he reacts to this guy. You'd think it was somebody cool like Bill Gates or something.

"I assure you, it's fine. Being in love makes you do foolish things." He laughs, throwing back his piece of hair, then waving good-bye and heading back toward the Paris.

"Of all the people to throw water on." Rand grunts, pacing around the fountain.

"Rand, he's just a guy. He puts on his polyester pants just like you do," I assure him, not wanting this to ruin our night together.

"You're right. I'm sorry," he says, shaking it off. "Aspen, have you ever been kissed next to the Eiffel Tower?" Rand asks, making my whole body tingle.

"I think I'm about to be," I reply, losing myself in his arms.

"That was our best kiss ever," I whisper dreamily to Rand. I just know that I will be replaying it in my head all night.

"I think all of our kisses are the best ever," he replies sweetly, stifling a yawn. I don't take the yawn personally since Rand spent the day subjected to Angel.

We are strolling hand in hand down the Strip from the Paris to Pirate's Cove. We are taking our time soaking up the sights, and each other. My cell phone rings and I groan, not wanting anything or anybody to interfere with this magical night.

"We'll always have Paris." Rand sighs, dreading the interruption as much as I do.

"Forget it. It's probably just a telemarketer."

"You'd better answer it. It might be something about Emerson."

I nod my head in agreement and dig my phone out of my Dooney. I don't recognize the number and can't help but get excited, wondering if maybe Rand is right. It would be awesome to wrap this case up and get back to our spring break.

"Hello."

"Hey, Aspen. It's Autumn. I got roped into going clubbing at Illusions's under-twenty-one club. I need a buffer. Please come?" she begs.

"Tonight?" I ask, checking the time on my phone and remembering Rand's yawn. It is already almost ten o'clock. Rand sulks off to watch the volcano explode in front of The Mirage.

"Please, Aspen?"

I consider the desperation in Autumn's voice over

Rand's humped-over shoulders. Normally, I would never choose anything over Rand. But he'll probably just go to bed. I don't want to miss out on a chance to get some clues about Emerson.

"I'll be there in ten," I say, hanging up.

⊚

Rand and I flash our IDs at the burly bouncer outside the club Slush. He rolls a red stamp that reads LOSER over the top of Rand's hand. Rand rolls his eyes at me, not appreciating the club's humor. When I told him that I was going clubbing with the girls, he suddenly perked up and wanted to come with me. So now I've got the best of both worlds.

Rand moves over to the imposing door separating the club from the hotel atrium. I can feel the bass vibrating under my kitten heels as the bouncer uses green ink to stamp LEGAL on the top of my hand. Slush employees seem to have an interesting way of interpreting Nevada state law when it comes to minors consuming alcohol.

"No way." Rand pouts after seeing my hand. He opens the door and we move into the club.

"Who cares? You don't even drink," I remind him. Last semester, Rand took advantage of just about every fraternity party on campus. He kept showing up at my dorm sloppy drunk, thinking I was in love with his psycho roommate. Eventually we decided that he shouldn't ever touch alcohol again.

"Yeah, but it just looks cooler." He laughs.

The club has three levels with a giant staircase running through the middle of each floor. The bottom floor is for dancing, the middle for sitting, and the top section is for VIPs only. Each floor has a mirrored bar with hundreds of bottles of liquor, and giant machines churning out the club's signature drink, slush. The icy concoction flows in a rainbow of colors down clear tubes and out taps on the bar.

I spot Autumn waving from the second floor and drag Rand upstairs. Autumn scoots over in the black leather booth to make room for Rand and me. Catrina is there, sipping blue slush delicately with a straw, her gloved hands in her lap. The corners of her mouth turn up in a smile when I introduce Rand. He holds out his hand and Catrina's smile turns into a terrified look. I lower Rand's arm gently and whisper that I'll explain later. The Dakota twins giggle and bat their eyes shamelessly at him, making him squirm.

"Aloha," Miss Hawaii greets him, which the twins think is hilarious.

"So are you telling him hello or good-bye?" Miss North Dakota slurs, clearly under the influence of the peach slush in front of her. Miss Hawaii ignores them and goes back to chatting with Miss Florida about the declining honeybee population and the devastating effects it could have on their home states' fruit exports. I can tell from Rand's stoic expression how taken aback he is that these girls are more than just pretty faces. Well, except the twins.

"Hi. We're the Dakota twins," North and South singsong, as if reading my mind.

"Are you really twins?" Rand asks, clearly confused by how this would be geographically possible.

"Sisters from another mister," they shout with glee, and then bolt out of the booth and head toward the dance floor.

Rand and I are laughing so hard that we can barely give the waitress our drink order.

"What's good?" I ask Autumn.

"I'd recommend anything but the kiwi slush because it makes you do that." My eyes follow her finger, which is pointing over a balcony and down to the dance floor. An out-of-control Lacy is dressed in a hot pink corset and purple miniskirt flipping her blond locks around like a maniac.

"Two Cokes, please," Rand tells the waitress after spotting Lacy. "Is that girl on meds?"

"She probably should be." I laugh, watching unsuspecting clubbers get assaulted with her deadly strands.

"I wonder if she gets to call Pageant Mistress *Mom*?" Autumn wonders aloud. We all laugh and for a split second I feel guilty that I haven't been completely honest with Autumn about my intentions for entering the pageant. She is a really nice girl and I hope that she isn't too mad when she finds out the truth.

"I really hope you win, Autumn," I say genuinely.

"Oh my gosh. That's the sweetest thing ever but I don't have a shot next to you."

"You guys should totally kiss now," a male voice says. I am about to smack Rand when I look up to see Lucas and Angel standing at our booth.

Angel looks like she has a lighthouse shoved up her butt she is beaming so brightly. Obviously she is still on her engagement high.

"You can't say shit like that once you're married," I remind him. I introduce Lucas and Angel to Autumn. Angel, who has never been one for common pleasantries, extends her left hand toward Autumn. She turns it ever so slightly so that the lamp above our booth catches her new bling. She is so predictable.

"Get over yourself," I say, busting her out. "Lucas and Angel got engaged tonight."

"Congratulations," Autumn tells Angel, shaking her hand.

"We'll be on the dance floor," Lucas announces, whisking off his new fiancée.

Rand and I exchange a glance, both still unable to believe those two are ready to make a lifelong commitment to each other. Just the other day at the airport gift shop Lucas refused to buy the jumbo pack of chewing gum because he was afraid it would last too long and he would get sick of it.

"I bet she ran off to be one of those mail-order brides," I hear Miss Hawaii say.

"Who?" I ask, curious.

"Emerson. I bet she got on a plane to Russia."

Highly unlikely.

"One of my friends did that once. She met some guy on the Internet who told her that everything was duty-free. So she took off to get all of us Prada purses, then the guy, like, kidnapped her and made her marry him. I never did get that purse," Miss Florida babbles.

Lucas and Angel may be crazy enough to walk down the aisle but Emerson doesn't strike me as the kind of girl who could be lured to the altar with the promise of a duty-free purse. Now a hayride and some s'mores, maybe.

Rand covers his mouth to hide a yawn. My cell display shows it is already midnight. As fun as it is watching Lacy make an ass out of herself and trying to anticipate what insane thing is going to come out of the twins' mouths next, I'm not getting any clues and rehearsal is just hours away.

"We are going to pack it in, ladies," I say, bumping Rand's leg with my butt to get him to scoot out. He smiles at me, obviously relieved.

We say our good-byes and look out over the dance floor for Lucas and Angel. They aren't easy to miss considering they are in the middle of the dance floor doing some serious dirty dancing. Most of the other people on the dance floor have just stopped and are gawking at them.

"Oh, lord," I say, pulling Rand toward the stairs. "Let's grab Swayze and Baby before they get arrested for public indecency."

Nine

"Are you freaking kidding me?" I say, my words completely sleep garbled. The blurry red numbers on the bedside alarm clock say 4:13 A.M.

"Pageant Mistress is furious that you aren't down here yet. Please hurry, Aspen," Autumn says, out of breath.

"Tell her not to get her Spanx in a bunch. I'll be there when I get there." I flip my cell phone shut and curse the day I laid eyes on Emerson Chambers. Then I see Mona curled up in the bedspread on the floor clutching a teddy bear I saw in Emerson's suitcase. If I went missing, I'd sure want someone like me to find me. Does that even make sense? Part of my brain is still back in the dream I was having of Rand and I strolling along a Parisian street. I can almost smell the fresh-baked bread coming from a café. I groan and pull myself out of bed. Carefully, I step over Mona. I look to Angel's bed and am not surprised to find it empty. I'm sure they are spending the night celebrating their engagement. Hopefully it is still premarital sex they are having.

I pull on some shorts and a tank top after pulling my hair into a ponytail. I grab my key card and head downstairs to the auditorium. I ride the elevator down with some other pageant contestants and we grunt greetings at each other.

Pageant Mistress is standing at the door with her ever-present clipboard. I have to fight the urge to grab it from her and beat her senseless for interrupting such a first-class dream. She truly is demented.

"Thanks for joining us, Brooks. I hope it wasn't too much trouble," she smarts off.

"Listen you washed-up, second-place loser, I'm on to you. So you don't want to push me too far," I hiss, surprising myself. I never have been much of an early riser.

Pain washes over her stunned expression. Just as quickly it is replaced by anger. She grabs my arm, hard. "It's not too late to cut you from the pageant," she threatens. I pull my arm back and stare holes through her.

"If you ever lay a finger on me again, you are going to be eating that clipboard," I warn her. She's crazier than I originally thought. I'm really going to have to watch my back today. While I don't think she would jeopardize the pageant by making me disappear, you can never fully anticipate what someone with such deep issues will do.

And I so don't want to end up walking the plank of the giant pirate ship out front.

"Did you just threaten my mom?" Lacy says, coming up behind me. Even at four in the morning her hair is still coiffed perfectly in a psychotic beehive/mullet.

"I was merely educating her on what happens to people who threaten me. But I guess you already know all about that, don't you, Lacy?" I remind her.

"Why are you even here? You don't care about winning the pageant," Lacy points out.

"Now that's just not true," I say sweetly. "I think I'll make a fine Miss Teen Queen." I saunter off to find Autumn, fairly certain that I can hear them growling behind me.

☺

"Please tell me that this is a joke," I say, surveying myself in a full-length mirror backstage. Autumn covers her mouth with her hand, trying to stifle a laugh.

"I never realized how bad it was until seeing it on someone else."

"Everyone who knows me is going to be watching tonight. I will never live this down," I say, nearly crying. I already know that my parents would have contacted everyone who has known me since birth to tune in tonight. And knowing my parents the way I do, I can just imagine that they are having some sort of party at our house. I picture Mom, Dad, Detective Malone, and even our mailman dying of laughter when I appear onstage in a skintight white jumpsuit complete with rhinestones and cape, white pleather shoes, and worst of all, a black wig with sideburns.

"Well, we are supposed to look like Elvis," Autumn says, picking up on my desperation.

"I want to die," I say, sinking into a director's chair. The other costume, a gold sequined slip dress, isn't so bad. But the Elvis one has me wondering if maybe I should just bail on the whole thing. I haven't been this fashionably challenged since sporting my mom's horrible hot pink prom dress to try to win back Rand's heart. At least I got him. What the heck am I going to get for dressing up like the King in front of the entire nation?

"At least you're in the back row now," Autumn points out. A fact I still had yet to point out to Rand or Angel. They are both totally expecting to see me front and center but I haven't had the guts to tell them it isn't happening.

"I suppose that is a plus," I say, wanting nothing more than to burn this outfit. My cell phone vibrates on the table in front of me. I pick it up and read the display. It's Harry. He always seems to have some freaky sixth sense about me.

"I've gotta take this," I tell Autumn, who smiles and walks away.

"You don't even want to know the things I'm putting myself through," I answer. Harry immediately starts chuckling.

"I was starting to wonder about you. I've been keeping one eye on CNN just in case," he teases. Even after two takedowns he is still a bit skeptical of my sleuthing powers. I think he just thinks I'm lucky.

"I'm in beauty pageant hell. My sadistic pageant director has me cross-dressing," I whine, pulling the wig off and tossing it on the table in front of me.

"And to think I wasn't going to tune in tonight. Hold on a sec, let me set my TiVo."

"Why do you get so much amusement from things that cause me pain? I thought we were past that point."

"I'm just teasing. I really was getting a bit concerned. I tried to follow up with Detective Grant but I haven't been able to reach her. Have you two found out what happened to Emerson?"

"Detective Grant is way too busy making herself hideous to bother with an investigation. She's totally giving me the runaround, but that's okay because she is in for a big surprise tonight." I laugh, making a mental note to try to dodge Pageant Mistress for the rest of the day so hopefully she forgets I haven't told her my talent yet.

"What about the hotel surveillance tapes?" Harry asks.

"No search warrant," I tell him, defeated.

"Oh man. You sound like a uniform now, Aspen. Since

when do you need a search warrant to get your hands on anything you want?"

"Are you insinuating that I should use my girly charms to illegally obtain evidence?" I tease.

"As an officer of the law, I could never suggest such a thing, but we both know that you could sell ice to an Eskimo if you really wanted to."

"Ah, so true," I agree. While I'm sure Rand won't be too hot on the idea of me trying to entice some lowly desk clerk, he'll just have to understand that there are some things I just have to do to get clues about my case.

I hear Pageant Mistress screaming through her bullhorn that talent rehearsals are about to begin.

"Harry, I gotta go. Hell's calling," I say, reaching back with one arm to unzip my hideous Elvis costume.

"I would think you would be completely in your element." Harry laughs.

"I'm starting to realize that when it comes to beauty, I'm just an amateur." I click off and hurry out of my costume and back into my rehearsal clothes.

"I know you think I've forgotten about your talent, Brooks, but I can guarantee you that I haven't," Pageant Mistress says, sneaking up behind me.

I force myself not to jump, knowing she meant to scare me. I spin on my heel and face her, not backing down an inch.

"I've been looking forward to it," I lie.

"Great, then you can go first," she says, huffing off.

Panic fills me as I realize that I can't show her the real talent I'm planning. I look around at all the other girls grabbing their tap shoes and batons and warming up their voices. Miss Hawaii is in the corner practicing some serious martial arts moves. Crap.

"You could always use Emerson's talent," Autumn whispers in my ear. She must have seen the sheer panic on my face.

"That's a great idea, Autumn," I say, yanking her up in a hug.

"Don't thank me just quite yet," she says, half-laughing. She walks behind our lighted vanity and returns holding a rope in one hand and a giant stuffed cow in the other.

"Why me?" I whine.

"She is the state lasso champion." Autumn laughs, handing me my new talent.

"I'm going to end up with rope burn," I say, not believing that I have to follow in the footsteps of a cow-patty throwing, 4-H joining, tractor-loving lasso champion. Could Emerson have been more anti-girly?

"Good luck, Aspen," Autumn says sincerely, disappearing to go warm up her legs for her ballet dance.

I take a long look at the rope in one hand and the stuffed cow tucked under the other arm. How hard can this be? The hole in the rope or lasso, whatever, is pretty big. And this cow is good-sized, too. This is going to be a breeze. I disappear behind the curtain for a few practice throws.

I set the cow down on the floor and slowly start to swing the rope around in the air. It's heavier than I expected and my upper body has never been particularly strong. I keep it slow at first, afraid I might jack myself in the face with the heavy rope. After a few seconds, I get the hang of it and swing faster. I'm actually pretty good. How embarrassed would Emerson be if she saw how good I was after just a few minutes of practice? I've so got the swinging the rope part down so now I throw it out to lasso the cow. The rope lands about three feet away from the cow. Okay, so maybe I need a bit more practice.

I gather the rope back up and start swinging again. I let it go and this time it grazes one of the cow's ankles. I giggle with glee at how easy this is. I bet Rand would think this is so hot. Maybe I'll have Autumn take my picture with my cell phone and send it to him.

"Brooks, get your scrawny butt out here," Pageant Mistress screams. No, she didn't just call me scrawny. I have so been called worse by better. I can't wait until this pageant is over.

I grab the adorable cow and my lasso and scurry onstage. As soon as the other girls see me carrying the lasso they move farther back. Autumn flashes me an encouraging smile.

"Wow, so you're going to copy Emerson's talent. How original of you," Pageant Mistress smarts off.

"It's a tribute to her," I lie. I can hardly wait to see the look on her face when I pull a switcheroo at the talent portion tonight.

I don't miss her eye roll at my reply. What I wouldn't give for a couple of minutes alone with her and my Dooney in a dark alley.

"Let's get this show on the road. Turn on your cow," Pageant Mistress orders, fully recovered from my statement.

Whatever. Wait. What?

Turn on my cow? I look to Autumn, who apologizes with her eyes, and then I trudge back over to the cow. I try to look like I know what I'm doing as I pick it up. I flip it over on its back to see a black ON/OFF button on its belly. I flip it to the ON position, just knowing my pseudo talent is about to take a serious turn for the worse. The cow comes to life with all four hooves moving and its mouth mooing continuously. I set it down on the stage and it takes off running. I stand there stunned, knowing I'll never be able to rope this heifer now. Every so often the cow stops and turns in the other direction, but never stops its annoying moo.

And to think I could be lounging at the pool sipping a mocktail while my hot boyfriend rubs sunscreen all over me. I've really got to stop getting myself into these situations, I think, while starting to swing my lasso.

By my third attempt, most of the girls are openly mocking me. Autumn is furious and trying hard to defend me.

"Moooove over, Aspen. It's time to let someone else practice their talent," Pageant Mistress says, nearly doubled over with laughter.

I chase my cow and turn it off. I act dejected as I head back behind the curtain. Let them all think they've got me figured out. They will be in for a huge shock tonight when I blow the judges away with my real talent.

"Are you okay?" Autumn asks, rushing back to check on me.

"I'm fine. I think I just need to practice some more." I feel bad lying to Autumn, since I'm positive that she would never have had anything to do with Emerson's disappearance.

"Are we done until the photo shoot later?" I ask, hoping that I've got enough time to solve this case and maybe get Emerson back onstage tonight so I don't have to humiliate myself in that Elvis costume.

"Yeah, nothing until three o' clock," Autumn says, waving good-bye while rushing back onstage.

I put the cow and lasso back, then hang up the routine costumes. I make a mental note to get my bikini, evening gown, and makeup ready as soon as I go back upstairs.

I check my phone and it is still only 6:30 A.M. I don't want to wake up Rand so I decide to treat myself to breakfast in the café.

I'm surprised at how many early risers there are, especially when I see Lucas and Angel among them. Then I notice that they are still in the same clothes they had on at dinner. Talk about your serious walk of shame.

"Hello, lovebirds," I tease, sitting down at their table. They both glance up, surprised.

"You have to go to rehearsal already?" Angel asks.

"That was over two hours ago. And I have suffered unimaginable humiliations in the last two hours," I say, grabbing a menu. I am so gorging myself on carbs.

"Thanks for sticking in there, Aspen," Lucas says, shoving a forkful of sausage into his mouth.

"You totally owe me another vacation, Lucas."

"Yeah, but next time we are totally getting our own room," Angel says, leaning her head on Lucas's shoulder. "Mr. and Mrs. Lucas Riley," Angel says dreamily.

"You guys didn't get married last night, did you?" I ask, nearly panicked.

"You know we wouldn't do that without you and Rand there," Angel assures me, sitting back up and taking a sip of her coffee.

"So, have you guys decided to wait?" I ask, crossing my fingers under the table.

"We are getting married this afternoon," Angel announces proudly. I paste a fake smile on while gripping the seat of my chair so that I don't fall off of it. Rand's voice whispers through my mind and I remember our conversation last night. This isn't my business. I can't control other people's actions, I remind myself.

"The ceremony is at 3:30 in the hotel chapel and it

will only take about fifteen minutes. They are fitting us in between Fergie and Josh, and some billionaire and his trophy bride," Angel beams. I can honestly say that I have never seen Angel so happy, not even when we were rescued from Lulu Hott's basement. Maybe she isn't making a mistake. Maybe Lucas is her future and her future is supposed to start right now. I smile again, this time for real.

"I'll sneak away from the photo shoot so that I can be there," I tell her, knowing there will be so much chaos Pageant Mistress won't even miss me.

I glance over to Lucas to give him an encouraging smile when I notice him suddenly looking nauseous, and I have a feeling it doesn't have anything to do with his breakfast.

☺

"Lucas doesn't want to get married," I tell a sleepy Rand. He closes his hotel door behind me and I plop down on Lucas's still-made bed.

"Then he needs to tell Angel that," he says, rolling back into bed.

"Rand, this is serious. Lucas is our friend and I don't feel comfortable letting him do something he doesn't want to do," I say, flipping on the light in between the two beds.

Rand buries his head under the covers. "I thought we talked about this last night," he mumbles.

"That was before I saw them at breakfast today. He about threw up when Angel mentioned that the ceremony is this afternoon."

"This afternoon?" Rand shouts, throwing off the covers. "I didn't think they were really serious. I thought they were just having fun on vacation and would come to their senses," he admits, running his hands through his serious bed-head hair.

"Oh, so now you think it's serious," I say, swinging over to the side of the bed and stomping my foot on the floor. "I've been running around like crazy trying to find a missing pageant contestant, rehearsing routines to perform on national television, and stopping my best friends from exchanging vows prematurely. I'm exhausted, Rand. I could use some help," I yell, instantly feeling guilty. I'm not mad at Rand, just all of the people who seem to get between us.

"I'm sorry, gorgeous. From now on, I'm going to handle Lucas and Angel, so don't worry about them," he promises, joining me on Lucas's bed. He wraps his arms around me and squeezes, coming in for a kiss. Even with his foul morning breath, I can't resist.

"Rand, you just don't know the things I've had to endure. Do you know that I had to try to lasso a fake, moving cow this morning? It was beyond humiliating," I say, burying my face into his chest.

"Holy crap. You with a lasso? That's hot." He laughs,

then finds my mouth to show me just how hot he thinks I am.

⊚

I use my key card to get back into my room. I'm surprised to find Mona still curled up on the floor. I can see her back heaving in and out and I realize that she's crying.

"Mona, what's wrong?" I ask, touching her shoulder. She turns over, startled, and starts wiping furiously at her tears.

"I'm fine, Aspen," she lies.

"You are clearly so not fine," I tell her, gesturing to the bed. She struggles to her feet, still clutching Emerson's teddy bear. She sits down delicately on the edge of the bed like she might break it.

I throw open the shades to let the bright Vegas day in and take a seat at the desk. Mona shields her eyes with a frail hand. Upon closer inspection she looks almost emaciated.

"When is the last time you ate?" I demand.

She turns her head, clearly ashamed. "A few days," she says softly.

I immediately pick up the room service menu and call down to order enough food for three.

"I'm so embarrassed," she says, a flood of tears running down her face again.

"I told you, Mona. Everybody has hard times. It's nothing to be embarrassed about." Her shame nearly breaks my heart as I remember how embarrassed my own mother was when I found out about all the credit card debt she had amassed.

"This trip was our last hope. What kind of mother lets her kid go to Las Vegas to be pimped out in a beauty pageant just so she can win money?"

"She knew she had a good shot at winning. Emerson is a beautiful, talented girl. I think that is why Pageant Mistress kidnapped her."

Mona's mouth drops open and her eyes bulge out.

"Aspen, do you have proof?"

"Not yet, but you are going to help me with that. After you eat your breakfast," I tell her, getting up to gather all the things I'll need for the pageant in a central location so that I can grab them at the last minute. I have a feeling my day is going to be jam-packed trying to solve a mystery.

Ten

"What are we doing again?" Mona asks me, for the third time. This is why I don't have a sleuthing partner.

"We are trying to use our feminine wiles to get the desk clerk to give us access to the security video," I tell her again, trying not to roll my eyes.

We casually approach the marble desk of the front lobby. Behind the desk is an exquisite mural of a treasure map and a huge treasure chest with jewels dripping out of it. A beefy guy who looks about twenty barely looks up from his computer as we saunter to the counter.

"Excuse me, sir. I was wondering if you could help us," I ask him, batting my eyes and pushing my pouty lips out a bit. He looks up with a blank expression, then points to a corridor off to the left.

"Why are you pointing?" I ask him, dropping my best sex kitten expression.

"I figured you wanted to know where the spa was," he says, lost again in his computer screen. I throw a disgusted look at Mona, not believing how stupid this guy is.

"I could care less where the spa is. I need some help trying to find a diamond necklace that my friend lost," I say, gesturing to Mona. She makes a good show of fingering an imaginary necklace and looking despondent.

"She is pretty sure she lost it walking from her room to the elevator. So we need to see the hotel surveillance tapes from that specific time," I tell him.

He finally looks up and laughs. In my face. I want to smack him really bad.

"We can't let you do that." He smirks.

"Why not?" I demand.

"Because there might be things on those tapes that a little girl like you shouldn't see," he says, covering his mouth to fake cough to cover his laughter.

Images of making out with Rand in the elevator come flashing back and I realize that a lot of people probably don't stop themselves like we did.

"Eww . . ." I say. Mona starts giggling, probably more out of desperation than anything else.

"They made us watch hours of security tape for training purposes, and some of the stuff will mess you up for life," the clerk says seriously.

"Okay, I'm going to be straight with you," I tell him,

leaning over the counter. "My friend's daughter is the pageant contestant who went AWOL. We are hoping that video will give us some indication of where she went or with whom." I slide back down on my side of the counter while the desk clerk seems to think it over.

"They've got that place locked up tighter than Fort Knox," he whispers, looking around. "I could get fired."

"You could also get a date with a beauty pageant contestant," I promise, not bothering to tell him it won't be me. His eyes light up and I notice that he is actually pretty cute and could probably get the date on his own, but I don't volunteer that information.

"Give me your cell phone number and I'll call you if I can pull it off," he says, punching some keys on his keyboard to make it look like I'm just another guest he's helping. He slides a slip of paper in front of me with a pen and I write down my digits. I flash him a smile and drag Mona away.

☺

"You can charm anything out of anybody, can't you?" Mona asks, amazed.

"He hasn't done it yet," I say, but not doubting that he'll be calling soon.

"What next?" Mona asks, obviously deluding herself into thinking that she is going to be riding shotgun with me all day.

"I need you to rest up. Tonight is going to be crazy. I'll call you if I get anything from the surveillance video. I'm probably just going to rehearse a little bit more today," I lie, feeling guilty. Mona starts to sulk off like a beaten puppy.

"Mona, wait a minute," I yell. She turns back, her eyes wild with excitement. I dig through my Dooney for my wallet and take out five twenties. I hand her the bills, which she takes reluctantly.

"I need you to scour Las Vegas for the best souvenirs you can find," I tell her.

"What kind of things do you like?" she asks excitedly, happy to have a task.

"They aren't for me. They're for Emerson. I'm going to find her for you by tonight," I promise her. She grabs me up in a hug then disappears into a sea of tourists.

I try not to wonder if I just lied to a desperate woman.

⊚

"Update me on the status of Operation Kill the Wedding," I ask Rand, while visually soaking up the sights of the Strip. We are riding in the back of an unusually clean taxi on our way to a cybercafé. Pirate's Cove has Internet access but I didn't want to take the chance of a pageant girl seeing me cyber-spy on Pageant Mistress.

"I can't find them anywhere. And neither one of them

will answer their cell phones," Rand reports, looking dejected.

"It's okay. Not everyone is cut out for detective work," I tell him, squeezing his knee. While I don't want to see Lucas and Angel get married, they are the least of my worries right now. I'm on a mission to dig up as much dirt on Pageant Mistress as possible.

"Are you going to pull it off this time, Aspen?" Rand asks, voicing the same question I've been asking myself all day. I shrug my shoulders and fall into him.

⊙

"I don't even want to know how many people had that up their nose before you got it," I tell Rand, laughing at the plastic tubes hanging from his nostrils.

"You've gotta try this. I feel like I just drank six Red Bulls," he says, kicking back in a lounger to enjoy more of his pure oxygen. The only Internet café we could find also doubles as an oxygen bar. So while I'm Googling, Rand is sucking up the purest air he's had since birth.

"She's like a ghost," I say, pounding the keyboard, which elicits a finger wagging from the tech support/oxygen bartender guy. "How is it possible that a person isn't Googleable?"

"Maybe that's her married name," Rand offers, not opening his eyes.

"No, I asked around. She's never been married. Apparently Lacy came from a sperm bank."

"Ouch, she must have serious issues," he says, readjusting his nosepiece. I have a brief flash of Rand at ninety hauling an oxygen tank behind him.

"Yeah, and she takes it all out on her hair." I laugh. I actually haven't had a problem with Lacy since our confrontation. I kind of feel sorry for her for having such a psycho mom.

I switch to Yahoo!, even though I know if anything is to be found, Google would have done it. Then I remember a website that my parents love to cruise now that I've introduced them to all things technological. It's a website that lists any crime a person has committed. It's an Illinois site but I'm sure Las Vegas must have one too. I switch back to Google and type in "Las Vegas Municipal Court Cases." I'm quickly linked to a site that allows me to type in Pageant Mistress's real name. Within seconds, I see that someone has been renewing a restraining order against her for several years. Unfortunately, the records are sealed, so I can't find out who wants Pageant Mistress a hundred feet away from them at all times. It proves she is obviously crazy, or at least one other person thinks so, but it's still another dead end.

"I can't do this again," I admit, defeated.

Rand sits up in his lounger so fast that the plastic tubes get ripped out of his nose.

"Don't ever say that. You're the smartest person I've

ever met. If anybody can figure out what happened to Emerson Chambers, it's you," Rand says, gripping my shoulders.

"But what if she just walked away and I've wasted our entire vacation looking for her?"

"Do you really believe she just walked away?" Rand asks, searching my eyes.

"No, I really don't," I admit.

"Then that settles it. We won't stop looking until we find her." He grabs my hand and kisses the top of it. Then he grabs the plastic tubes and places them in my nose. I start to protest but he holds me against him for a few minutes. When he finally releases me, I'm invigorated and ready to beat down every hotel door on the Strip if I have to in order to find Emerson.

My cell rings on the way back to the hotel. I don't recognize the area code and am instantly excited, hoping it's my lucky break.

"This better be good," I shout into the phone.

"It's Paolo," the male voice says back.

"I don't know a freaking Paolo," I say, getting ready to hang up. Rand snickers beside me, knowing how irked I get when people waste my precious minutes. Why am I cursed to be the only teenager who doesn't have unlimited cell phone minutes?

"The desk clerk from Pirate's Cove," the voice shouts. "Get over here quick if you want access to the surveillance tapes. The guys take a break in fifteen but they are only gone for ten minutes." I click off without even re-sponding.

"There's an extra twenty if you get us back in ten min-utes," I say, tapping the cab driver on the shoulder. I dial Autumn's cell phone number as the cab driver kicks it in.

"Hey, Aspen," Autumn answers.

"Autumn, I need you to do me a really big favor and not ask any questions. Find the Dakota twins and have them prance around onstage in their swimsuits for about half an hour," I tell her hurriedly. The cab is pulling up in front of the hotel. Rand looks sad as he hands the cab driver two twenties.

"No problem, Aspen. I'll give them a ball of yarn or something. They'll be up there for hours." She laughs. "And I'm assuming I'll get to ask about this later?"

"Only if everything goes as planned," I tell her, hop-ping out of the cab. I click off and rush Rand to the front desk. Paolo is nervously waiting for us.

"Who's the dude? I can only take you," Paolo says, avoiding Rand's eyes.

"I'm the boyfriend, dude. And Aspen doesn't go any-where without me," Rand clarifies.

Paolo nods his head briefly in understanding. I feel sort of guilty jeopardizing his job and all. I totally have to get him hooked up with one of the girls before I leave.

"They only leave for ten minutes," Paolo says, a thin layer of sweat forming on his forehead.

"I know how to get them to leave for longer," I say,

winking at Rand. "Just tell them that the Dakota twins are rehearsing in their bikinis."

A smirk crosses Paolo's nervous face as he picks up the phone. He dials a number then waits patiently as someone picks up.

"Holmes, I just got a tip that some Grade-A T & A is on display in the auditorium. You want me to hold down the fort for you?" he asks so convincingly that I may have just thrown up in my mouth. Rand has to walk away because he is laughing so hard. Paolo hangs up the receiver.

"Did you have to be so vulgar?" I reprimand him.

"Hey, it had to be convincing, right?" He slaps Rand's outstretched hand. I kick Rand in the butt but it doesn't even faze him because I'm only wearing flip-flops.

"I'd better be getting some good clues to put up with this despicable display of testosterone," I huff, slipping behind Paolo into a stairwell hidden in the treasure map mural.

⊚

We slink up three flights of narrow steps in a deserted corridor. My heart is pounding louder than my footsteps. Rand keeps looking behind him every five seconds, making me even more nervous.

"If anybody spots you, act like you're foreign," Paolo offers. Oh yeah, like that's going to work. I'm like the quintessential American girl.

As we climb the fourth flight of stairs Paulo stops on the landing and gestures to a gray door. He opens the door, which turns out to be a tiny janitor's closet. He gestures for us to get inside. Rand and I are pressed together like a peanut butter and jelly sandwich as Paolo shuts the door. Everything turns pitch black and Rand uses the opportunity to grab my butt.

"Cut it out, Rand," I whisper, swatting his hand away. Two male voices start bellowing outside the door and I'm certain that we are totally busted.

"Come on, man. I don't want to miss this. I've been trying to catch these girls half-naked all week. Those stupid monitors don't show nothing," a voice says, hurrying past our door. I hear someone else grunt in agreement. A few seconds later, Paolo flings the door open and the light nearly blinds us.

"Come on, you've only got ten minutes," he says, practically drenched in sweat.

Rand and I untangle ourselves and rush through the open door next to the closet we were in. I don't know what I was expecting a hotel surveillance room to look like, but it wasn't like this. This place looks like it could launch the space shuttle.

"Whoa," Rand says, his eyes flitting around the hundred television monitors on one wall of the room.

I sit down below the screens at a wall-length desk full of lights, buttons, and elaborate-looking machinery. This is going to be a little more difficult than rewinding a VCR tape like I had imagined.

"How do you work this stuff?" I ask Paolo, who looks near heart failure.

"I don't know. I thought you knew," he says, nearly bursting into tears.

I want to punch him but I figure he is already torturing himself enough. I look to Rand, hoping that he will be able to help even though he doesn't even know how to text message. He shrugs his shoulders helplessly while continuing to gaze around at all the screens.

"Aspen, look. It's Lucas and Angel in the café downstairs," Rand shouts excitedly, pointing to one of the screens. Sure enough, the lovebirds are feeding each other french fries.

"Get down there and stop that wedding," I demand. Rand flies out of the room and down the stairs. Paolo continues to guard the door even though I'm pretty sure he would just pass out if anybody actually showed up.

I find the screens for the cameras in the auditorium and on one can see two guys hiding in a back corner ogling the Dakota twins, who I can see on another screen are onstage doing tae bo in their bikinis. I so owe Autumn.

I look back to the control panels. Okay, obviously this thing is like a big DVR. I just have to find out how to get it to pull up the surveillance from the day and time I want. Of course none of the buttons have labels. A man must have designed this place because it makes no sense. I sit down in a wheeled desk chair and start sliding down the panel looking for anything that might jump out at me. Finally, I just start pushing buttons. Paolo starts to say something, then just shakes his head and goes back to guard duty.

The buttons I pushed are making some of the cameras focus in so well that I can tell what bra Angel is wearing. None. Gag me! I spin to the middle of the console and start messing with some of those buttons. Two screens go fuzzy and then I see new footage come on. I recognize Lacy and some of the other trophy wives sneaking some coins in a slot machine. Gross, Lacy is totally wearing the same outfit she had on yesterday. I glance down to the time/date stamp and realize this footage is from last night. Okay, I guess she isn't as foul as I thought.

"You've only got about five minutes," Paolo announces.

I check the auditorium screen again and the two guys don't look like they are going anywhere for a while. I move back to the button I pushed to bring up Lacy and push it a few more times. Rand and I making out in the elevator flashes up on one screen. As embarrassed as I am that at least two security guys saw this, it is still kind of hot. Paolo clears his throat and I hit the button to go back a few more times.

A screen displaying the café downstairs catches my

eye. Pageant Mistress is sitting at a booth chatting amiably with one of the pageant judges. The time/date stamp tells me this was the morning of the day Emerson disappeared.

Emerson appears in the corner of the screen and walks toward the booth. Pageant Mistress slides a fat envelope across the tabletop and the judge discreetly hides it under his palm then tucks it into his jacket pocket. Emerson covers her mouth in horror after witnessing the entire transaction. Pageant Mistress smiles smugly, oblivious to Emerson running from the café.

So, Emerson saw Pageant Mistress paying off a pageant judge. Would knowing she definitely wasn't going to win the pageant be enough to make her take off?

I hit the button a few more times to fast-forward it to later that night.

Onscreen, Pageant Mistress sashays through the lobby like she owns it then stops suddenly to talk to someone. I can't see who it is so I try switching views to another camera. I end up screwing it up and focusing on one of the guest floors instead. I see Emerson walking down the corridor wearing the black cocktail dress that was missing. She seems to be wiping tears off her cheeks and looks very despondent. But also very alone. She disappears into the elevator.

I hit a few buttons trying to adjust which camera footage I'm seeing, but it won't give me what I need. I pound my fist on the control board in anger. Suddenly the angle of the camera switches and I can see the back of the person that Pageant Mistress is talking to. A tall man wearing a funny hat. That's all I can see.

"Turn around," I will the man in the tape. Actually I can't even deduce that it's a man. It could be an Amazonlike woman dressed in a pantsuit. I fidget with a few more buttons and see Emerson exiting the elevator into the lobby.

"Oh my God, they're coming," Paolo says, rushing back into the room and slamming the door behind him. He looks around frantically for a place to hide. I glance up to the screens and realize that he is right. The men didn't stick around for the Dakota twins' finale. I hear their voices closing in on us and I hit the button to restore all the screens to the current hotel activity. I bolt out of the chair and grab Paolo. I slam him against the wall and bury my face against his neck. He smells like cotton candy. Not nearly as good as Rand but he doesn't make me want to hurl either.

"What the . . ." the voices say in unison.

I jump back, acting shocked and embarrassed. "You said we'd have this place all to ourselves," I say, play-slapping Paolo's arm.

"Uh, sorry," he manages to squeak out. We both bolt for the door and I hear the guys giving him high fives from behind me. I don't breathe easier until we are down all four flights of stairs and walking through the treasure map mural again.

"I think I need to change my pants," Paolo says, gripping the lobby counter for support.

"I owe you big-time," I tell him, wiping the sweat from my palms onto my jeans. I wave good-bye and disappear around the desk into the casino.

©

I head to the café to help Rand round up Lucas and Angel and talk some sense into them, very quickly. The hotel is filling up with local newscasters getting ready for the pageant tonight. I recognize the pageant emcee, some cheeseball pseudo-celebrity who is the announcer on a reality show. He blinds the cameras with a fake set of choppers that are bigger than my grandma's falsies. Lacy blindsides him and starts shaking his hand, trying to kiss up. She's too stupid to realize that he doesn't have anything to do with the actual judging. Not that she really has anything to worry about now anyway since Pageant Mistress paid off at least one judge. The emcee tries to gently shove her out of his limelight but she isn't having it. I crack up as I weave through the reporters to get to the café.

Rand is standing next to a chalkboard announcing the day's specials, wringing his hands.

"Where are they?" I ask, confused.

"I lost them," he says delicately, sensing I'm not going to be happy.

"This day is not going well," I say, collapsing onto a bench outside the café. Rand sits down next to me and wraps his arms around me.

"You couldn't find anything on the surveillance video?"

"Just Emerson leaving her room by herself and Pageant Mistress talking to someone wearing a ridiculous-looking hat. Not exactly *CSI* clues, but I did see Pageant Mistress pay off a pageant judge."

"That's something. Couldn't you use that against her?"

"I suppose. But I've been thinking: Why would Pageant Mistress go to all the trouble of kidnapping Emerson if she has already paid off the judges?"

Rand nods his head in agreement as he considers this. My brain hurts so bad from trying to get inside the mind of a psycho ex-beauty queen. And I thought Lulu Hott was bad.

I haven't been this tired since last semester, when I was trying to figure out what happened to Harry's niece. I went forever without a solid lead, which isn't easy for an instant gratification girl like me.

"Maybe you should just concentrate on yourself. Everything will work itself out," Rand says, trying to comfort me. I wish I could believe him, but deep down I feel like sometimes my actions keep the world running smoother. If it wasn't for my brilliant detective skills, Lulu Hott would never have been caught and would still be running around terrorizing people because she got dumped on homecoming, and Charm would be in graduate school scoping out a new roommate to off to get straight A's. I have to solve this or Mona may never know what happened to her daughter. But how?

I've tried everything I can think of. And without any help from Detective Grant, my resources are pretty limited. She is so going to pay for not helping me.

"Rand, come on. I need some things from that boutique at Illusions," I say, yanking him off the bench and out onto the Strip.

Eleven

"I need some serious concealer," I tell the clerk.

"Sweetie, you look fine," she assures me.

I start laughing hysterically. "No, it's not for me. It's for a woman I'm going to be doing a makeover on. She's got more luggage than Louis Vuitton." I laugh.

"How sweet of you to help her feel better about herself," she says, handing me a tube of what looks like flesh-colored spackling.

I hand it to Rand then proceed to scour the boutique for other things I might need. I pick up a spare pair of hose because I always manage to poke a nail through them no matter how careful I am. I hand him a cordless curling iron that will be perfect for Detective Grant's onstage makeover.

I'm nearly giddy thinking about how I'm going to

trick her into coming onstage. She'll be super PO'd at first, but when she sees the miracle I've worked, she'll definitely thank me.

I grab some mousse and an adorable pink baby tee with the hotel logo for myself. I've so earned a souvenir. I shell out nearly the last of my cash to the clerk while Rand waits outside in the hotel atrium for me.

"Good luck with your makeover," the clerk offers, handing me my purchases.

"You should tune in. It'll be live on Channel 8 tonight," I tell her, and then leave her open-mouthed to find Rand.

I find him staring up at the creepy memorial for Cleve Lynn's deceased wife.

"I feel really sorry for him," Rand says sincerely. "He has billions of dollars and he couldn't even save his wife."

I glance up at the large portrait of the crocodile-skinned woman and feel a chill run down my spine. I can't shake the feeling that she looks familiar—probably because I've been here before, but I felt that way the last time too.

"I'd be lost without you, Aspen," Rand says, bending to kiss my cheek.

"Don't worry. I use sunscreen so I won't ever suffer her demise," I tell him, leading him away from the memorial before I get creeped out any more. We jaywalk across the Strip back to our hotel and up to my room.

"I'll meet you at the chapel at 3:15," I tell Rand, giving him a kiss.

"I look forward to seeing you in that dress," he says, kissing my neck.

"Rand, focus. I have to make myself gorgeous, stop a wedding, find a missing girl, win a pageant, then we can make out," I tell him, pushing him away even though I don't want to.

I slide my key card in the slot in the door and blow him a kiss good-bye.

Mona is sitting on one of the beds surrounded by I LOVE VEGAS T-shirts in a rainbow of colors, fuzzy dice, and snow globes full of miniature Las Vegas attractions.

"Anything?" she asks breathlessly.

I shake my head. Her face drops as she gets up to put on the dress she has laid out for the pageant.

"I really am trying," I tell her, upset with myself that I don't have any clues. I almost tell her that I saw Emerson leave her room of her own free will but I still don't accept that someone else wasn't involved in coercing her down to the lobby, especially since Pageant Mistress was there at the exact same time.

"I know you are, sweetie. If there is anything I can ever do to repay you. You know, as long as it doesn't involve money." She laughs halfheartedly.

I drop my bag on the bed and reach for her to give her a hug. It's the least I can do.

"I'm nervous about tonight," I confess, something I didn't even tell Rand.

"You'll be great. Emerson would be proud to have you taking her place," she says, patting me on the back.

"I guess I'd better go get ready," I tell her, suddenly tired and wishing I could get another fix of that pure oxygen.

@

I shower slowly, the scalding water cascading over me, attempting to wash away some of my stress. I'm so happy that I've got all my favorite hair and body products and don't have to use that foul complimentary hotel stuff anymore. How can they consider something complimentary if its sole mission is to attack your hair follicles?

After drying off and slipping into a tracksuit, I gather up my makeup, gown bag, and hair supplies. I'd much rather get ready in my hotel room but Pageant Mistress is making us all get ready backstage. I reach for the black stilettos that I'll be wearing at the pageant tonight. A tiny note flutters out of one of the shoes. I bend down to pick it up, immediately recognizing Rand's handwriting. *So you don't break a leg*, the note reads with an arrow pointing down. I flip the shoes over to see that he has covered the soles with some sort of skid-proof stuff. He is officially the sweetest person on the planet. I tell Mona goodbye and trudge downstairs to the auditorium.

The stage and seating area are filled with people running wires and placing cameras just so. I thought I was nervous before but now I'm petrified. Images of me tripping on a wire when they announce my name fill my head. And what about the entire nation seeing me in that Elvis costume? I feel ill.

Why do I have to be cursed with the ability to sniff out trouble? Why can't I just be satisfied to live a boring life like other people? I guess there is no sense in beating myself up. I can't help it, I'm just gifted, even if it feels more like a curse sometimes.

I drag my stuff up a hidden set of stairs on the side of the stage and push the curtain back to enter the backstage area. A cloud of aerosol fumes immediately assaults me. I put my gown bag up to my nose and mouth as I try to make my way to my vanity.

"No wonder there is a hole in the ozone," I tell Autumn, who is made up beautifully.

She laughs but doesn't take her eyes off the liner she is using to trace her lips. I lay my gown bag over the top of my chair and set my makeup on the vanity. I wave my hand in front of my face a few times trying to recirculate some fresh air. It doesn't help, considering an average of ten girls are keeping their trigger fingers on their hairspray nozzles at all times. A constant cloud of hairspray hangs in the air just waiting to assault my pea-sized lungs. This crap is so bad for my asthma. I feel around in my makeup bag for my spare inhaler, just in case. I've learned that lesson the hard way a few times in the past.

"Aspen, can you help me?" Catrina asks, holding out some flesh-colored Jell-O–looking blobs.

"What are those?" I ask, horrified, backing away from the wiggly mounds in her gloved hands.

"Give them here," Autumn says, putting down her lip liner. Before I can figure out what they are Autumn shoves them into Catrina's strapless bra.

"Thanks, Autumn," Catrina says, waving a gloved hand and disappearing back to her vanity.

"Isn't that kind of like cheating?" I ask.

"I don't have a boyfriend." Autumn laughs.

"Very funny. I meant in the pageant."

"Nope. You're allowed to use any and all enhancements for the pageant," she says, sitting down on a stool to pull on her panty hose.

I look around and notice girls putting on fake eyelashes, colored contacts, and clip-in hair extensions. One girl even shoves something down the back of her underwear to make her butt look rounder.

"I haven't washed my hair since Tuesday," Miss Iowa yells over her shoulder. I fight the urge to gag myself. Who could go that many days without washing her hair and why would she want to?

"Oh yeah? Well I haven't washed mine since Sunday," Miss Connecticut counters.

"Eww . . ." I whisper to Autumn.

"Dirty hair holds styling products better," she informs me.

I'm still beyond grossed out. I watch in fascination as an already bronze Miss Wyoming applies self-tanner perfectly. I tried that once but just ended up with orange palms.

"I think we are the only natural ones here," I tell Autumn, still gazing around just waiting for a girl to attach a prosthetic limb or something.

"Actually . . ." She laughs, flashing me. Her nipples are covered with these giant X-shaped Band-Aids. It's freaky looking.

"What the . . ."

"They're called Low Beams." She snickers.

"I don't get it," I say, cringing because all I can think about is how bad it would hurt to pull those suckers off.

"You know, they keep it really cold in the auditorium and I don't want the entire nation thinking I'm a porn star."

"Oh, right. Low Beams. I get it." I laugh. "Wow, all this time I thought I was a beauty guru. I feel like a total amateur," I admit, watching Miss Rhode Island slather on more foundation even though she's already wearing more layers than my mom's seven-layer salad.

"You don't need any of that crap. You're beautiful just the way you are, but you'd better haul ass if you are going to do anything with your hair." She laughs, spying my hair cascading sloppily from a hair clip.

She's right. I've been standing around here gawking like an adolescent boy instead of primping. I'm going up against human Barbie dolls so I'd better get to working my Clinique.

I spread out all of my trusty products, applying them a little thicker than normal so they show up on camera. After I'm done with my face, I start on my hair. I've decided to make smooth, wavy, loose curls parted to the side like an actress from the forties. I don't go crazy with the hairspray like the other girls, knowing that if I did, I'd end up looking like I was wearing a helmet after prancing around with that Elvis wig on. They'll be lucky if they aren't all sporting ponytails for the evening gown portion. I always wait until last to put on my lipstick so I don't end up eating it. I coat my lips with the brightest shade of red the boutique had. I take a look in the mirror and can't help but smile at what I see. I'm a total showstopper. Even though Pageant Mistress stuck me in the back row, I bet the cameramen are going to be all over me.

"Nice lipstick," Lacy smarts off, as she breezes past in nothing but a push-up bra and a thong.

"Ever heard of a Brazilian?" I reply. She shrieks then scurries back to her side of the stage and wraps a towel around herself.

"This experience wouldn't have been nearly as fun without you, Aspen," Autumn says, slipping into her gold slip dress for the first routine.

"The two of us definitely don't fit in here," I tell her.

"The things people do for money," Autumn says, suddenly sounding ominous.

"You can always get a student loan," I remind her.

"I wasn't really talking about me," she says, checking her watch.

"Who were you talking about?" She's got me curious with her sudden switch of demeanor.

"It's nothing. Listen, I've got an errand to run. Can you tell Pageant Mistress I'm in the bathroom if she comes looking for me?" She dashes off before I can even answer.

I check my cell phone to see how much time I have before Angel is supposed to get married. I'm sure Rand has handled everything but I still want to make sure they didn't pull a fast one and get married at a drive-thru this afternoon.

I pull my new panty hose out of the bag of purchases I made at the Illusions's boutique today. I manage to actually pull them on without incident. I can't help but wonder where Autumn rushed off to in such a hurry. And I forgot to ask her if she ever remembers seeing Emerson talking to someone wearing a funny-looking hat.

I pull on my gold sequin–covered slip dress and slide into my safety stilettos. This outfit is way better than the Elvis one, but is still pretty cheesy. I can't help but think that this dress is something that dead lady from the creepy memorial would wear.

I'm ready with time to spare. I feel kind of bad not sticking around to cover for Autumn but I decide to head up to the wedding chapel early. I think I remember Angel saying something about being sandwiched in between a billionaire and Josh Duhamel. He'll probably dump Fergie when he sees me in this dress. I glance around to make sure nobody is paying attention, then slip out of the corner of the curtain.

I slither past some camera people who are too busy setting up their live feeds to even notice me. I take the stairs even though these heels are already killing me, because I don't want to take the chance of being spotted by Pageant Mistress. I kick my heels off and head up four floors. That should be enough to avoid anyone who knows me. I pull open the door and enter a corridor full of guest rooms. I follow the signs to the bank of elevators, hop on an empty one, and take it straight up to the top floor.

When the elevator doors open I'm stunned to see Autumn sitting in a velvet wingback chair sobbing her eyes out. Something tells me this isn't just pre-pageant jitters.

"Autumn, we really need you now," a male voice booms. I can't see who it belongs to because I'm still standing frozen in the elevator. I jump off just as the door dings that it's about to shut.

Autumn looks up, seeing me for the first time, and looks a bit like a deer in the headlights of a semi. She buries her face back into her hands, letting more tortured sobs escape. This male voice is wanting Autumn to do something that she really doesn't want to do. But what?

"Autumn, please. It'll be fine," the male voice says again.

This time I turn toward the voice to see who it is coming from. I get that dizzy feeling that I'm becoming quite accustomed to when the pieces of a mystery start snapping into place in my mind. A familiar face. A funny-looking hat. Autumn's comment about people going to extremes for money.

I rush past the man decked out in the black tuxedo and into the hotel chapel. The pews are covered with white silk bows but don't hold any guests. I rush to the rose-covered altar and throw up the veil of the girl standing there. Just as I suspected: Underneath the white tulle is Emerson Chambers.

☺

"Remember me?" I ask her, as if anyone could actually forget me. I can hardly contain my excitement at seeing Emerson safe.

"Please don't tell my mom," Emerson begs, tears streaking her perfectly made-up face.

"What? That you're alive and safe? She's worried sick about you!" I yell.

"I know. I hate that I had to disappear. But she never would have agreed to me marrying Cleve."

"No kidding?" I smart off. "Do you think maybe it's because he is going to have to be spoon-fed about the time you are graduating from college?"

"I had no other choice, Aspen. I knew that I wouldn't

win the pageant when I saw Pageant Mistress pay off a judge, and then Cleve came along and offered to save my family's farm. I couldn't let them lose everything."

"You are their everything, Emerson," I remind her. She gets giant tears in her eyes as the gravity of what she was about to do sinks in.

As soon as I walked off the elevator and saw Cleve everything started snapping into place. Minus the beef jerky skin and the cancer stick habit, Emerson is a total doppelganger of Jessie Lynn. That's why I thought she looked familiar when I saw her picture. The man with the funny hat talking to Pageant Mistress in the lobby wasn't wearing a funny hat after all, just a bad hairpiece. I wish I could have seen how obsessed Cleve Lynn was with replacing his dead wife the night that Rand and I ran into him. With his kind of money, he can pretty much buy whatever—and whoever—he wants.

"This isn't any of your concern, Miss Brooks," Cleve Lynn says, grabbing my arm. He starts to pull me out of the chapel. I fight back but he is surprisingly strong for a geriatric. I stomp on one of his fancy Italian loafers with my bare heel. He yells in pain and releases my arm. I bolt back to Emerson and beg her to leave with me.

"We'll figure something else out. I'll help you," I promise, trying to make her come to her senses.

"I've had about enough of your interference, you little pest," Cleve says, coming up behind me. He tries to grab my shoulders but I duck and he misses me.

"Come on, Emerson," I beg, ducking and weaving away from old man Lynn. He clamps a liver-spotted hand down on my arm and starts dragging me again. Where the hell is Josh Duhamel when you need him?

"I suggest you unhand the lady immediately," a familiar voice says from behind me. My bright red lips break into a huge smile. Who needs Josh? My knight in shining armor, Rand, is here. Surprisingly, Cleve doesn't loosen his grip on my arm.

"This doesn't concern you, son," Cleve says, pulling me toward the exit.

Rand does this mean karate chop thing to Cleve's arm and he instantly lets go of me.

"Don't you ever touch her again or I won't be responsible for my actions," Rand barks at him, while wrapping me safely in his arms.

"I can make both of you disappear in a heartbeat," Cleve threatens.

Another death threat? Stand in line. I'm so not even fazed by this guy, especially now that Rand is here. I just have to talk some sense into Emerson so she doesn't spend her life with a psychopath who wants her to be his dead wife's clone.

"The deal's off," Emerson says, handing Cleve a diamond as big as my earlobe. My mouth starts to salivate a little as the candlelight glints off the stone.

"You can't do this. I already paid you," Cleve shouts, getting right into her face. Emerson pulls the check out from the top of her Vera Wang wedding gown and hands it back to him.

"Aspen's right. I can figure out another way to get the money." She rips the check into a million pieces and throws them at Cleve.

"You are all going to regret the day you humiliated me," Cleve screams, a vein in his forehead bulging dangerously. He storms out of the chapel and out of our lives. For now anyway.

"I'm so sorry that I worried all of you," Emerson says, tearing the veil off and tossing it aside.

"I can't believe I was going to be your witness. You must think I'm such a crappy friend," Autumn mumbles, walking into the chapel.

"I never should have told you I was planning to marry Cleve. It wasn't fair to put all that on your shoulders," Emerson says, hugging Autumn.

"Let's go find your mom. She's missed you like crazy," I say, ushering everyone out of the chapel.

@

"Aspen, how can I ever thank you?" Mona cries, not letting up on her death grip of Emerson.

"Emerson could help me by taking her place back in the pageant from hell," I tell them.

"I don't even remember the routines," Emerson says over her mother's shoulder.

"Oh, I'm just kidding," I lie, feeling guilty for wanting to rip Emerson away from her mother after they just found each other again.

"We'd better get back or Pageant Mistress is going to freak," Autumn says, grabbing my arm.

"Right." I sigh, exhausted. I can't help but feel like there is something I'm forgetting though. I found the missing pageant contestant. Reunited her with her mother. Ran off the old geezer billionaire looking to marry a clone of his dead wife. Marry. Hmm . . .

"Oh my God! Lucas and Angel!" I scream, grabbing Rand and bolting back to the elevator. "How could I have forgotten the whole reason why I went up there in the first place?" I cry, knowing that we are going to be way too late to stop the ceremony.

"You should be proud of yourself, Aspen. You solved another mystery. Harry is going to freak and your parents won't believe it. If Lucas and Angel make the mistake of getting married, it isn't your fault," Rand assures me, squeezing my hand.

"Then why does it feel like it is?" I ask him, mentally screaming at the elevator doors to open.

When the doors finally open, what seems like an eternity later, Rand and I spill out of them, desperation lacing every step. I'm rounding the corner to the chapel when I see them.

Lucas looks like an ad for Ralph Lauren in his gray tuxedo with white cummerbund. Angel is wearing a skintight white jersey dress and a tiara (as if I couldn't have seen that coming) and is holding a bouquet of ivory roses. They don't have to say a word because the smiles on their faces tell us everything.

Twelve

"Oh my God," I shout, collapsing into the velvet wing-back that Autumn was occupying just a half hour ago. I bury my hands in my hair, then just as quickly pull them back out again, remembering that I am going to be on television in about an hour.

"It is what it is," Rand says, shrugging. I throw an evil glance his way. He knows I hate it when he says that.

"We didn't get married," Angel announces, tossing her bouquet onto a cherrywood table.

"Nope," Lucas verifies.

"Oh thank God," I say, bolting off the chair to hug Angel.

"I thought you were all for us tying the knot," Angel says, pulling back to study my face. Crap. Lucas ratted out my plan of fake proposing. What a jerk.

"Thanks a lot, genius," I say, kicking at Lucas with my heel.

"I'm innocent, dude," Lucas swears, holding his arms, palms out, up in the air.

"Do you honestly think I can't spot one of your scams a mile away?" Angel asks, fixing her lipstick in a nearby mirror.

"What was I supposed to do? Let you turn out like Britney Spears?" I defend myself.

"You're a good friend, Aspen, but sometimes you might not know what is best for everybody."

I fight the urge to tell her how incredibly mistaken she is. Besides, it doesn't really matter. Angel and Lucas realized they were much too young to commit themselves to each other for life. Case closed. Actually, since Emerson isn't missing anymore that would be the *second* case closed.

"Aspen found Emerson," Rand says, reading my mind.

Angel and Lucas both suck in their breath waiting to hear what they obviously think is horrible news.

"Chill out, guys. She was about to pull an Anna Nicole but we got there in the nick of time," I say.

Lucas looks horrified and Angel keeps doing the sign of the cross over her pushed-out chest, even though I know for a fact she isn't Catholic.

"You shouldn't talk ill of the dead, Aspen," Angel says, giving me a stern look.

"I wasn't saying anything bad about her. Listen, you guys should just be happy that I found her when I did," I point out. You just can't please some people.

"I don't understand why she would want to overdose on drugs," Lucas mumbles, looking forlorn. Angel grips his arm reassuringly.

"She wasn't trying to overdose on drugs. She was going to marry a really old man," I clarify, rolling my eyes.

"You don't always have to talk in riddles," Angel scolds me.

I look up at Rand, who is covering his mouth so that a laugh doesn't escape. *These two are so made for each other,* I tell him with my eyes. He walks over and wraps his arms around me. Suddenly I feel very tired. Like bone tired. Like there is no way that I can perform tired.

Rand wraps his arms around me tighter, and whispers in my ear, "You don't have to do this."

I'm about to agree with him when I remember how bad Autumn needs money for college. If I don't show up the pageant will be cancelled. I know that Lacy is probably going to win because of her mom paying off the judge, but if Autumn has even the teeniest chance of winning, I have to show up. Besides, if I don't show up, I won't get to have my revenge on Detective Grant. Just imagining the look on her face when I pull her onstage for a makeover gives me the boost I need to get moving.

"Can we trust you two not to do anything life altering in the next few hours?" I ask Angel.

"Very funny. Actually, we are going to spend the rest of our night in the front-row seats at the pageant that Rand reserved for us," Angel smirks.

My stomach rolls at the thought of my friends watching me perform. Then I remember nobody will be able to see me since Pageant Mistress stuffed me in the back corner. The whole ordeal is so humiliating that I still can't bring myself to tell them the truth.

"My little cheering section," I say, faking excitement.

"Good luck, Aspen. Not that you'll need it," Angel says, giving me a squeeze.

"Knock 'em dead, wench." Lucas laughs, smacking my butt. Rand grabs his arm and acts like he is going to break it.

"She's my wench and don't you forget it." Rand laughs.

"Speaking of wenches, I'd better get to the auditorium before Pageant Mistress hunts me down," I say, waving good-bye to Lucas and Angel, and giving Rand a peck on the lips before disappearing into the elevator.

⊚

"I hate you with the intensity of a thousand suns," Pageant Mistress tells me through clenched teeth.

"Wow. Why don't you sugarcoat it a little bit," I say, cheesing it for the photographer.

"You're a spoiled, self-centered, smart-ass little bitch," she says, not holding back.

"I prefer 'beyotch.' And you seriously need to get a grip. If you piss me off, I might be tempted to skip the whole gig. And we both know what happens if you lose Miss Illinois," I threaten in a sweet voice.

She mumbles something unintelligible then walks away. If only I could find a way to get back at Pageant Mistress for being so horrible, this vacation wouldn't be a total loss. Unfortunately I'm just too tired to cook up another scheme so I'll have to let karma deal with her.

After sitting through endless photo ops, I finally get to head backstage to freshen up. I check my hair, which still looks amazing, and then reapply my lipstick. Lacy comes up behind me and bumps my arm, which causes a tragic red streak across my cheek.

I wish I had the energy to beat her down but I don't. I turn around slowly to see her with her fists out, ready for action.

"I feel sorry for you, Lacy," I tell her, genuinely meaning it. "Your mom has used you all these years to try to succeed where she never could. I hope you find the strength to stand up to her someday." I turn back around and start to gently wipe away the lipstick streak while trying not to destroy my makeup. I can see Lacy in the mirror, just standing there stunned. After a few seconds, she finally walks away, looking defeated.

"I just threw up," Autumn says, coming up behind me wiping her mouth on her hand.

"Please tell me you brushed your teeth," I say, surprised that she would be so nervous.

"I'm really sorry that I didn't tell you about Emerson," Autumn says, near tears.

"It's okay, really. I respect you for having so much loyalty to Emerson. Even if you do smell like puke," I say, laughing. We give each other a quick arm's-length hug so that we don't mess each other up before going onstage for our beginning routine.

"Are you ready for this?" Autumn asks, following me over to the edge of the stage. I try to peek out the corner but someone has tied the curtains back so nobody can see in or out. I can hear a booming voice counting down to ten, and then the emcee's voice comes on welcoming everyone to the 50th Annual Miss Teen Queen Pageant.

"Well, I was," I answer, fairly certain that my stomach is no longer in my body.

"Good luck," Autumn says, blowing me a kiss and rushing off to her place in our alphabetical-by-state lineup.

I've never done yoga, but I try to breathe in a few slow, deep breaths. The line keeps getting shorter and shorter as girls disappear onto the stage to walk out and introduce themselves. Oh, why can't I be from Wyoming, I think, as only two girls remain in front of me.

What am I saying? This is a piece of cake. I've taken down a psycho homecoming queen bent on revenge, a girl so obsessed with a 4.0 GPA that she'd practically kill for it, and I just foiled the plans of a billionaire to clone his dead wife. I can so do this.

What am I worried about a few television cameras for? This is going to be a breeze. Heck, I might even win. Now that would be the karma that would bite Pageant Mistress right in the butt!

"Miss Illinois, Aspen Brooks," the emcee shouts, busting into my reverie. I snap to and head out through the slit in the curtain. I smile all the way up to my eyebrows. This is going to be fun. Maybe I'll even want to get into pageants professionally after this.

Uh, maybe not. I'm blinded by white-hot lights as I make my way to the stage, trying not to trip over the thousand wires all over the place. I try to keep my head up and my smile pasted on as I carefully make my way to the emcee. Luckily, the lights are so bright onstage that I can't really see the hundreds of people in the auditorium.

"Tell us a little bit about yourself, Aspen," the emcee says, thrusting a microphone in my face.

"I'm a freshman at State University," I say, a little shaky. "Where I'm a Beta."

"Whoo. Whoo. Whoo. Go Betas. Go Betas," I hear Angel's unmistakable voice scream from somewhere out in front of me. It gives me a boost of confidence knowing that I have three of my best friends cheering me on.

"In my hometown, I'm famous for solving mysteries. My boyfriend's name is Rand Bachrach and his family owns Bachrach Chocolates. I plan to become a defense attorney someday. And my favorite color is pink." The emcee moves the microphone away before I can finish, which irritates me to no end.

"Good luck tonight, Miss Illinois," he says, robotlike. The audience starts clapping and some music starts playing and I know I'm supposed to move to my place in line now because Pageant Mistress told us that like a thousand times. But I can't help it. I just have to give my parents a shout-out.

I grab the emcee's microphone and yell into it, "I love you, Mom and Dad." The crowd goes wild and I shove the microphone back at the emcee just as he is practically baring his fake teeth at me. I skitter into line behind Miss Idaho and listen to the rest of the girls introduce themselves. None of them pull a stunt like I did; they just allow themselves to be cut off mid-sentence. So I can guarantee I already made a huge impression on the judges.

Most of the girls are so nervous they can barely speak. Others seem to have been hired by their local tourism council to promote their states, which is kind of nauseating. I crack up when Miss Maine gets onstage and accidentally admits she's allergic to lobster. It continues with Miss New Mexico swearing she saw a UFO hovering over her local Kmart. As if a higher life form is actually going to come all the way to Earth and not at least go to Target!

I wonder if it's possible to fall asleep standing up? I think so because the next thing I remember is hearing Miss Wisconsin start to list different kinds of cheddar before being cut off. Finally, Miss Wyoming hits the stage in pigtails begging people to come to the last frontier. I'm still kind of in a daze when the lights change and the song to our first routine comes on. My body seems to go on automatic pilot.

I kick when I'm supposed to kick. Spin when I'm supposed to spin. And generally put the cast of *So You Think You Can Dance* to shame. It's over before I know it and we are heading backstage for a costume change.

Backstage is like a free-for-all. Sequin dresses and heels are flying everywhere. Girls are flying around half-naked. Autumn and I huddle in a corner and change into our swimsuits.

"This is a trip, huh?" I ask. We both start giggling as a topless Miss Iowa takes a stiletto to the forehead. She stands there dazed for a minute then puts on her bikini top backward.

"Should we tell her?" Autumn asks.

"Nah." We take turns spraying each other's butts with this stuff football players use to grip the ball better. The last thing I need is a cheek springing loose on national television. I assess myself in the mirror and I look totally smoking in my Burberry bikini. I was afraid that Pageant Mistress was going to assign us all some nasty black one-piece to wear but I know she was too interested in showing off Lacy's twin assets to make her wear a one-piece.

I pull my hair up and reapply my lipstick then head back to my place in line. I'm not even nervous this time. Who cares if millions of people are about to see me in a bikini? There's only one I care about and he's got a front-row seat.

"Miss Illinois," the annoying emcee shouts as I walk through the curtain pretending I'm a supermodel. I decide to go with kind of a pouty sex-kitten look this time. Until I hear Rand yell, "Now that's what I'm talking about." Then I just kind of crack up and adopt a goofy smile. I swivel my heels around perfectly to give them a good view of what my momma gave me, then make my way back next to Miss Idaho.

It wasn't as boring watching the other girls come out this time because I liked trying to guess what type of suit they would choose to wear. I totally nailed Miss Minnesota's fur-trimmed bikini but I have to admit I did not see Miss Nebraska's one-piece made entirely of corn husks coming. It's a good thing there isn't a breeze in the auditorium or Miss Nebraska's suit would have shucked itself right off her.

I'm starting to feel a little self-conscious going with such a safe bikini choice. Some of the other girls have really gone all out to show their love for their state. It's not that I don't love Illinois, I'm just not about to don a beard, top hat, and red-white-and-blue bikini to remind everyone that Abraham Lincoln, my personal fav president, totally hailed from Illinois. Some of the girls are taking the whole state thing a little bit literal though. Especially Miss Rhode Island, who trots out wearing a bikini the equivalent of two tiny circle Band-Aids and a triangle-shaped bottom all attached with dental floss. Okay, we get it. Rhode Island is the smallest state in the Union.

Finally, Miss Wyoming hops out on her stick pony (why wasn't I informed we could use props for the bathing suit competition?). I have to admit that her bikini made from red handkerchiefs, cowboy hat, and cowboy boots looks adorable. I am definitely out of my element with this crowd. If only I'd had more time to prepare for the pageant instead of trying to figure out what happened to Emerson. Oh well, I'll just have to knock them dead in the talent portion. Which I just know I will.

Miss Wyoming finishes her final hop to the end of our line and we all smile and wave at the audience while disappearing one-by-one backstage. Bikini tops and bottoms start flying and it is impossible to shade my eyes from all the girl parts. These chicks don't have a self-conscious bone in their bodies. I rush over to my vanity and start changing into the ridiculous cowgirl outfit that Emerson was going to wear for her lasso routine. I've got everyone fooled into thinking that I'm still going to humiliate myself by going onstage and trying to lasso a stuffed animal. I check my cell phone for the time and realize that Detective Grant will be here soon. I have to stall her long enough to get her onstage for my talent.

I made sure to tell Emerson to stay away from the pageant so that Detective Grant wouldn't realize that I had found her. I know it's kind of mean to deceive her, but she will thank me after she sees what she could look like with just a little effort. I fire up my cordless curling iron, knowing that I won't be able to spend a lot of time on her hair but even a few curls in that rat's nest will be an improvement.

"Oh my God. Somebody stole my ballet slippers," Autumn cries, near hysteria.

"Wait, are you sure?" I ask her, checking around her stuff.

"They were just here and now they are gone," she says, slamming her hand down on the vanity.

I check around in my own area and I notice that Emerson's lasso is gone.

"My lasso is gone too," I say, knowing immediately who the culprit is. Pageant Mistress. She still thinks she can throw this thing in Lacy's favor. How sweet it will be when she realizes that I won't need that stupid rope for my makeover talent. I dig around in my bag and find the ballet flats that I was using to practice with.

"Can you use these?" I ask Autumn, holding up the shoes. She grabs them and stuffs her feet in them. They look about two sizes too small but by the look on her face she's determined to make them work.

"But what about you? What will you do with no rope?" she asks, genuinely concerned.

"Don't worry. I've got it covered." I grin.

⊚

I'd say that the talent portion of the competition is kind of a bust. So far, we've had one near concussion (Miss Connecticut, who was juggling chain saws and dropped one on her head), one performance eerily similar to that Michael Jackson Pepsi commercial gone bad in the '80s (someone really should have told Miss Delaware not to be tossing around a fire-tipped baton with so much product in her hair), and one vomiting episode (Miss Tennessee volunteered to be the choking victim for Miss Arkansas's CPR demonstration and apparently she got a little too aggressive with her thrusts). Pageant Mistress can barely wipe the grin off her face.

I'm skirting the outside of the auditorium searching for Detective Grant. I don't even let myself think about how screwed I am if she doesn't show up. Some guy in a ball cap grabs my arm as I walk by. I know I look adorable in this cowgirl outfit, but please!

"Get your hands off me," I warn, pulling my arm from his grip.

"Aspen, it's me," Detective Grant's voice says from under the ball cap.

"Why are you dressed up like a guy?" I ask. Looking

unkempt is one thing, but deliberately making yourself look like the opposite sex? She's just begging for my help.

"I, um, just don't want anyone getting suspicious," she says cryptically. I'm about to ask about what, then decide I really don't care.

"The note is in my purse backstage. You'll have to come back there with me," I say, heading through the backstage entrance.

"Wait. I'm not allowed to go back there," she says, weirdly trying to disguise her voice.

"Don't you want to help find out who was threatening Emerson?"

Her eyes dart around suspiciously then she falls in behind me. We climb the stairs to the back of the stage but before I pull the curtain to slip through I stop.

"It's pretty crazy back here. I'm just saying . . ." I warn her.

"I remember," she says, following me through the curtain. Girls are running everywhere trying to find clothing and shoes. It seems that Pageant Mistress has been very busy collecting souvenirs from every state.

"The lady running this thing is a loose cannon," I explain to Detective Grant. She keeps her head down the whole time. I hear Miss Idaho doing her onstage performance of one hundred ways to prepare potatoes. She is on number ninety-six. I've timed this perfectly. I grab my Dooney off my vanity and make a show of going through it looking for the note.

"Oh, it was here. I just know it was." I pretend to get upset and wrap my arms around Detective Grant in a bear hug. Stunned, she actually hugs me back. Delicately, I feel around on her belt until I find what I'm looking for. I slide her handcuffs carefully off her belt, then grip them in my palm.

"Thanks. I needed that," I tell her, pulling away. Miss Idaho has just barreled through the curtain with her cooking cart. I hear the emcee announcing Miss Illinois to the crowd. I run back to my vanity and drop my purse. I grab my makeup bag and my curling iron. Detective Grant looks overwhelmed by all the action backstage and doesn't notice me sliding a chair onstage.

"The note is out here," I tell her, grabbing her arm and steering her toward the stage. She looks around confused by all the applause. She finally realizes that she is onstage with me but I push her into the chair and handcuff her arms behind her back before she can escape.

I run over to the emcee and grab the microphone away from him.

"There has been a little change in plans. I won't be performing the lasso routine but instead I'll be doing a five-minute makeover on someone who truly needs it."

I'm careful to switch off the microphone after I'm done talking because Detective Grant is threatening my firstborn.

"Do you have any idea how much trouble you are in? If you let me go right now, I promise not to press charges," she says, her face turning a very unnatural shade of crimson.

"Cut that out. Not even the best foundation will cover that up. You'll thank me for this later," I promise her, setting my makeup out on the floor of the stage.

"There is something you don't understand," Detective Grant says, almost pleading.

"I get it. You're scared that the guys at work won't take you seriously if you look like a supermodel. But I'm going to prove you wrong," I tell her, switching the microphone back on.

"Can the cameras get a before shot?" I ask, looking toward the camera with the red light on. One of the cameramen gives me a thumbs-up. I shake up my foundation, which isn't exactly the right tone for Detective Grant's complexion, but I'll just have to make do. Besides, anything is better than what she's showing the world now.

"Most people don't realize it," I tell the audience, "but our skin is our largest organ. It protects all of our other organs and it is very important to take good care of our skin." I stick the microphone in the crook in my arm and slather some super-expensive moisturizer on Detective Grant's face. I can almost hear her skin drinking it up.

"One of the biggest makeup mistakes that women make is to use the wrong shade of foundation. Has anybody ever seen somebody with that orangey telltale jawline? Eww . . ." The audience starts laughing as I carefully apply foundation to Detective Grant with a makeup sponge.

I try to ignore the look she's giving me as I'm kind of afraid I might actually melt if I meet her eyes.

"My subject has hazel eyes and brown hair so I'm going to play up her eyes with a tint of green with brown eyeliner," I say, carefully tracing on liner and then brushing on a small amount of shadow. I don't have enough time for a really intensive makeover so I'm trying to hit the highlights.

"When it comes to mascara, too much can be a bad thing. You don't want to end up with spider lashes," I say, carefully coating Detective Grant's top lashes. The audience is either asleep or mesmerized. I'm going with the latter.

"Blush should always be applied to the apple of the cheek," I inform everyone, pinching the center of Detective Grant's cheeks. I carefully brush on a light rose-colored blush.

"A lot of people think they can pull off dark lipstick, but it just isn't true. You have to have just the right look or you end up looking like a clown. It's always best to start out with a neutral color then gradually add color from there."

I can hear some whispering from the crowd and I know that it is because Detective Grant looks so awesome. I figured she had a decent base but who knew what lurked beneath this baseball cap. I pull off the hat and toss it aside. Her chestnut hair falls in a silky sheet to her shoulders. I grab my cordless curling iron and hurriedly make a few wavy curls. I know my time is about up and I want to make a strong impression on the judges. I'm standing in front of Detective Grant so that the judges and the audience can't get a very good look at her until I'm finished. I want to have the element of surprise on my side.

Her hair does exactly what I want it to, falling in thick curls around her head. I run my fingers through it then spritz a little product on. I stand back and can't believe what I've done. Detective Grant looks gorgeous, like supermodel gorgeous. And she's even smiling. I step out of the way so that everyone can see her and the crowd erupts into applause.

I'm so winning the talent portion of this pageant! The applause is so loud that I don't even hear the screaming at first. But I know that Pageant Mistress has got to be screaming because her mouth is wide open as she is running toward Detective Grant with a disturbing look on her face.

Before I can even react Pageant Mistress knocks the chair that Detective Grant is handcuffed to on its side.

"You! I can't believe you had to come ruin this for me too. I hate you!" Pageant Mistress screams. The cameramen quickly cut to commercial while several security guys rush the stage and grab Pageant Mistress. I unlock Detective Grant's handcuffs and help her up. I feel really bad. I mean, I knew that Pageant Mistress would be pissed about me switching talents but I didn't think she'd go psycho on Detective Grant.

"Hello, Andrea." Detective Grant sneers. "I'm pleased to tell you that you are under arrest for assaulting a police officer." She grabs the cuffs from me and slaps them on Pageant Mistress/Andrea's wrists. I can hardly contain my joy at the karma that seems to have bitten Pageant Mistress in the Spanx-covered buttocks. But how in the world does Detective Grant know Pageant Mistress?

"I'll deal with you later," she says to me. Then she directs the security guys to escort Pageant Mistress, who is screaming about being robbed of her crown, backstage. Even the prospect of serving a teensy bit of jail time in a hideous orange jumpsuit and germ-laden flip-flops can't wipe the smile off my face.

Thirteen

The rest of the talent portion of the pageant goes off without a hitch, unless you consider Miss Wyoming's horse taking a dump on live television a hitch. But after everything else that went down nobody really gave a steaming pile of horse crap much thought, except the camera guys who were forced to clean it up.

"Okay, ladies, get into your evening gowns quickly. We've got three minutes until we are live again," Lacy says, stepping right into her mom's stilettos.

I watch her as she tries to step on Miss Alabama's gown. Luckily, she misses or the gown would have been ruined. I want to kick her really bad. She catches me staring and I quickly glance away, knowing there is no way I have time to fix my hair if we get into another catfight.

Besides, I wouldn't want to take a chance on ripping the exquisite violet gown my mom made for me.

"Hey, Aspen," Lacy whispers, scooting up next to me.

"Yeah," I say, keeping my eyes on my mirror.

"I know you think since my mom's gone that you've got the pageant in the bag, but you're wrong. I'm going to be the next Miss Teen Queen no matter what," she practically growls.

"Okay, well, good luck with that." I snicker. Lacy huffs off, exasperated that I won't take her bait and fight her again.

Lacy's dislike for me is nothing but thinly veiled jealousy. People just naturally feel inferior to me. It's kind of a curse. Lacy is so threatened by me it isn't even funny. She's done everything but lift her leg and pee to show me that the pageant circuit is her territory.

"I thought you two were going to throw down again," Autumn says, having eavesdropped on my conversation with Lacy.

"Not hardly, I feel sorry for her. My parents have never made me do anything I didn't want to do. I can't imagine growing up like that. Who knows what her life will end up like." I feel a twinge of guilt that I haven't called home once since spring break started. Rand has talked to my parents several times but I just haven't had a chance to call. Autumn and I take our places in line, laughing at the swishing noises our gowns make getting there, which gives me the best idea.

I'm super nervous about the question portion of the evening. What if they ask me something stupid like if I'm against the death penalty or something? I crane my ear as close to the curtain as possible and try to hear the questions.

"What would you do to make the borders less penetrable?" the emcee asks Miss Delaware. Unfortunately for Miss Delaware, she thinks he is talking about Borders, the bookstore. I can't listen anymore because it actually hurts my brain.

I'm starting to wonder if they began giving the girls multiple choice questions because it is almost my turn already. But as nervous as I am, I really want to get this over with. Miss Idaho disappears onto the stage so I only have a few seconds. I have to admit this pageant thing isn't what I thought it was going to be.

I might not care for some of these girls but I definitely respect them. It takes guts to put yourself out there for the whole world to judge. Pageants are definitely not for the fainthearted. A part of me wishes that each girl here could win something but I know that isn't realistic. I just wish that fate would intervene so that the rightful girl gets crowned Miss Teen Queen.

Someone nudges my arm to indicate that it is my turn. I stand up as straight as I can, plaster a smile on my face, and walk through the curtain. I try not to squint at the blinding lights as I make my way to the emcee. I can't remember this guy's name for the life of me.

"Ooh, lady in violet," he says smoothly, which gets a laugh from the crowd.

"I'm wearing a Judy Brooks original," I say, which catches him off guard, but I swear I can hear my mom screaming at the television even though she's almost two thousand miles away.

"That's great," he says, careful to hold the microphone away from me so I don't steal his thunder. I can't help but stare at his teeth. They are so white that they almost look blue. He senses me staring and curls his top lip over them a bit.

"Miss Illinois—" He clears his throat then glances back to the note card he's holding. "—experts are saying that the Internet has had a negative effect on how people relate to each other. How do you respond?"

My first instinct is to be outraged. Who are the so-called experts who are spouting these lies? But I quickly collect myself, remembering that about a million people are watching me right now.

"I would have to say that I don't agree. I actually think that the Internet has made the world much smaller and has brought people closer together. I've made friends with people in other countries that I might never meet in real life but I still consider them friends because we share our lives with each other. I also think computer interfacing is an amazing resource for people who are too painfully shy for some social situations. They can sit comfortably in their homes while still interacting with people. And what about people who are disabled or disfigured in some way? The Internet allows them a nonjudgmental way to interact with others." I am just getting started when I hear this little dinging sound and the audience erupts in applause. I swear I can almost hear Rand whistling. I beam a smile in what I hope is his direction.

"Thank you for that surprisingly intelligent response," the emcee says, and then gestures toward the line of girls who came before me. I strut over to take my place in line next to Miss Idaho. I can't help but wonder if the emcee was being sarcastic about my answer.

After hearing the next three girls answer, I know that the emcee was actually being sincere. These girls are so nervous they are coming off like total brain donors. I feel guilty remembering all the times I thought pageant girls were all brain dead. While some of them are definitely a little light in the scholar department, most of them just get under these lights and in front of the cameras and freeze up. Luckily there isn't much that trips me up.

I struggle through the next forty-five minutes listening to unintelligible answers while trying to keep smiling. I'm fairly positive that my top lip is actually stuck to my teeth. I never realized looking beautiful could be so painful. We keep having to stop for commercial breaks and I'm about to go crazy. I can see the commercials in one of the nearby monitors. Hair Club for Men, Hoveround, and Metamucil. What demographic are they trying to target exactly? And would those people really be watching the Miss Teen Queen Pageant? I think not.

The audience is getting restless and people are escaping to the bathroom in droves.

Miss Wyoming approaches the microphone and I can almost hear the whole auditorium sigh with relief that the question portion of the evening is almost over.

"Miss Wyoming, would you say that you are living a 'green' lifestyle?" The emcee shoves the microphone toward a confused-looking Miss Wyoming. The answer must come to her because she suddenly starts beaming from ear to ear.

"Oh, I'm not a vegetarian." She giggles as the dazed emcee pulls the microphone back to announce another commercial.

"Thank you, Miss Wyoming." The emcee sighs. "Now it's time to let our contestants in on a little secret."

All fifty of us tense up while trying to keep our plastic smiles beaming. Surprise? What in the world are they going to subject us to now? Aren't the Elvis costumes bad enough?

"The girl crowned Miss Teen Queen tonight is going to be chosen by the American public. That's right, folks. All evening we've been flashing a telephone number and website across the screen for people to vote for their favorite contestant. The Miss Teen Queen Pageant is breaking new ground with this exciting development tonight. Stay tuned to see who America picks as the next Miss

Teen Queen." The emcee beams his bluish-white smile into the camera then it disappears as soon as the red light on the camera goes off.

All of the pageant girls scurry behind the curtain to change into our hideous Elvis costumes. All of the girls are giddy with excitement about the surprise voting shake-up, with the exception of Lacy, who just kicked some poor camera guy with her stiletto. She looks like she is actually snarling as she storms backstage.

"What's the matter, Lacy? Are you afraid the voting might not be fair?" I laugh. She doesn't bother looking up from her BlackBerry as she flips me off. I'm sure she's probably too busy voting for herself. My giggles are cut short as I glance at the hideous Elvis costume hanging over my mirror. I can't believe that I am voluntarily humiliating myself like this. I'd better at least place in the single digits.

I carefully slip out of my beautiful gown and hang it carefully over my vanity table. I squeeze myself into the white polyester jumpsuit, my body screaming at me the whole time.

"Does this make me look like I've got camel toe?" Autumn asks, adjusting her black Elvis wig.

"We all look like we've got camel foot in these things." I laugh.

"You've made this so fun," Autumn says, patting me on the back.

"I have to admit, this pageant stuff is a lot harder than

it looks." I carefully slip my wig on, checking to make sure my sideburns are even.

"I still feel guilty about Emerson," Autumn admits. She fidgets nervously with her rhinestone-studded belt buckle.

"You were just being a good friend. There were evil forces conspiring that hookup that you never would have stood a chance against," I reaffirm. I can hardly wait for the competition to end to find out what was going on with Detective Grant and Pageant Mistress. I hope that crazy beyotch rots in jail. If I can just make it through this last routine. At least we aren't using live animals like Pageant Mistress had planned. She had to drop the animals at the last minute when a tiger almost mistook Miss Florida for a T-bone.

Autumn and I hurry out to take our places onstage. I'm still stuck all the way in the back, not that Angel and Rand would be able to recognize me in this costume anyway.

"Rubbernecking" starts blasting as soon as we hit the stage. My arms and legs take on a mind of their own. I flash my first genuine smile of the night as I realize that I've gotten pretty good at dancing. The crowd seems to be singing along, which I take as a good sign. At least they aren't doubled over in their chairs laughing at our costumes. We wrap up the routine with a hundred jazz hands shaking in the air. All of the girls around me seem to let out deep breaths they've been holding all night, including myself.

"Let's give a big round of applause for the girls representing all of our fifty fine states," the cheesy emcee says, even though everyone is already clapping. He seems to sway off balance for a second then I see someone grab his microphone.

"Nobody puts Aspen in a corner," Rand's infuriated voice shouts. Then a tuxedo-clad Rand bounds toward me, grabs my arm, and drags me to the front row. The Dakota twins sigh dreamily at Rand and scoot over to make a place for me. Rand leans down and kisses me then rushes off stage before I even know what happened.

Everybody is oohing and aahing as I stand in a daze. Rand always catches me off guard with these occasional bad-boy moments. My cheeks flush (which so never happens) when it sinks in that Rand's PDA was just televised worldwide. I swear, I've got the most perfect boyfriend.

"The votes are being tallied by Pricewaterhouse-Coopers and we'll be back with the results after these messages from Colgate," the emcee announces. I'm positive he got a kickback from Colgate with those choppers. He throws me a dirty look as I exit the stage but nothing can kill the Rand buzz I'm on.

"Oh my God. Your brother is so hot. Can you hook us up?" the Dakota twins squeal. Autumn squats down and I'm pretty certain she has defiled her Elvis costume in a urinary way.

"Um, he's not my brother. He's my boyfriend," I explain, unzipping my costume.

"Oh. Can you still hook us up?" Miss North Dakota asks. I get a revelation right before I'm tempted to smack her for thinking unpure thoughts about my boy.

"I actually do have someone I could hook you guys up with. Let's get together after the pageant." They giggle and disappear to change back into their evening gowns.

"Who do you hate so much that you would hook him up with those two?" Autumn asks, wadding her Elvis costume into a ball and tossing it in a nearby trash can.

"Hey, you could sell that on eBay, unless it has pee on it." I laugh. "And those two aren't that bad. My friend will love them." I smile just thinking about Paolo, the desk clerk who helped me get into the surveillance room, and how excited he'll be at a shot with the Dakota twins.

I slide back into the perfect body-molding gown that mom made me. I'm really hoping my shout-out can get some interest going in her line of clothes. All of her clothes are totally amazing and she really deserves some recognition. I touch up my hair and makeup and head back to the line.

All of the girls are nervous about the results. Everyone wants to win so bad. I'm actually kind of ambivalent for the first time in my life. I don't really need to win like some of these other girls. It's kind of weird not feeling competitive to the point of wanting to grab the tiara off another girl's head. Maybe I'm just growing up a little bit.

The Miss Teen Queen melody is cued and we all strut out to the stage standing shoulder to shoulder. I can usually call these competitions from a mile away but with the phone-in/website vote component, it's anybody's guess. Slowly we all take each other's hands in a show of solidarity. Except Lacy, who ridiculously refuses to hold anyone's hand, therefore breaking our chain. I want to flip her off really bad but then I get a glimpse of Miss Arizona's ungloved hands and I'm truly speechless. I totally get the whole hand model thing now.

I look back to the crowd, which is still impossible to see because of the blinding lights onstage.

"Go Land of Lincoln," I hear Angel shouting from the right side of the stage. Angel's got this total celeb crush on Abe Lincoln, it's so embarrassing. But right now I'm not embarrassed, just proud that I have such great friends cheering me on.

"We're live from Pirate's Cove in Las Vegas at the Miss Teen Queen Pageant tonight. This envelope holds the future of one lucky girl. Miss Teen Queen wins twenty thousand dollars. She will also spend the next year traveling the United States as a role model for young girls all across the country. Before we crown our new queen, let's bring out last year's Miss Teen Queen, Miss Fawn Flora," the emcee yells enthusiastically.

Last year's Miss Teen Queen was a total scandal hound. She actually posted pictures of herself kissing another girl on her MySpace page. Then she got arrested for stalking

Jerry Springer. I think she's kind of mental. I mean, who stalks Jerry?

Fawn teeters out on toothpick-sized stilettos. She is crying so hard while trying to hold on to her faultily attached tiara that she has black streaks running down her face. She reminds me of the girl on the cover of Hole's *Live Through This* CD. It's not a pretty sight. Someone please hurt me if the highlight of my entire life is winning the Miss Teen Queen Pageant.

Fawn makes her way down the catwalk, waving to a crowd that doesn't sound so adoring. I think I actually hear somebody yell "crack whore" but I can't be positive. The emcee grabs her tiara as she makes her way back up the stage and somebody quickly escorts her off before it gets ugly.

"This is it. The moment we've all been waiting for," the emcee says, skimming some of the words on the teleprompter. I have to admit that I kind of like him for a second for trying to move this thing along.

"The fifth runner-up and winner of a one-thousand-dollar gift certificate to Omaha Steaks is Miss Wyoming." Miss Wyoming screams as a random, gowned woman throws a sash over her and hands her a single red rose. Steaks? Seriously? But Miss Wyoming is beaming like she won a BMW or something so I guess that's all that matters.

"The fourth runner-up and winner of a set of Louis Vuitton luggage is Miss Nevada." Lacy screams and runs backstage before she can be outfitted with her sash. She is so upset that I think I might have actually seen her hair deflate a little bit. It's not first place but LV luggage is nothing to sneeze at.

"The third runner-up and winner of an all-expenses-paid trip to New York City is Miss Illinois." I'm still mentally drooling over the luggage that Lacy won when a third place sash gets draped across my shoulder and I'm handed a dozen red roses. I won third place! And I'm excited about winning third place! I am definitely growing up. I hear Rand, Lucas, and Angel cheering for me and I wave in their direction.

"The second runner-up and winner of a guest spot on Laila Ali's new reality boxing show is Miss Arizona." The crowd goes wild as Miss Arizona displays a wave but I notice she already has her gloves back on. She lets them place the sash over her but refuses to take the roses for fear of getting stuck with a thorn. I don't think she is going to be trading jabs with Laila anytime soon.

"This year's Miss Teen Queen and the winner of twenty thousand dollars is Miss Louisiana." It takes a minute to register that Autumn is Miss Louisiana, but when it does, I scream for joy as the emcee roughly sticks the tiara on top of Autumn's head. She looks dazed, but in a good way. I'm psyched about the NYC trip I won but I couldn't be happier for Autumn.

Autumn strolls down the catwalk as we all get bathed in confetti. The lights in the auditorium go on, signaling that the show is over. Rand, Angel, and Lucas rush on-stage and give me a giant hug.

"Can we please go have some fun now?" I beg Rand.

"I thought you'd never ask," he replies, scooping me into his arms. I rest my head on his shoulder and close my eyes, knowing that my work here is finally done.

Fourteen

"Hello, Aspen," a familiar voice says as Rand approaches my hotel door.

"Make it go away," I moan, burying my face in his shoulder.

"That was quite the little stunt you pulled out there," Detective Grant says angrily. I can't help but notice as Rand delicately places me back on my own two feet that she hasn't removed her makeup or pulled her hair back into her face-stretching bun.

"You've got to admit . . . I've got talent," I say, touching a loose curl dangling against her shoulder. She flashes me a dirty look and jerks away.

"I can't believe you have the nerve to joke around when a girl is missing and possibly in grave danger. Where's the note?" she demands, getting all red in the face and completely disrespecting my makeover.

I kind of forgot to tell Detective Grant about finding Emerson. Pageant Mistress's stage rage totally blindsided me. I can't wait to find out what that was all about.

"Aspen already found Emerson," Rand pipes up, taking a defensive stance next to me. He doesn't like it when he feels like someone is threatening me. Rand has so got my back.

"What are you talking about?"

Instead of standing in the hall trying to convince her I just slide my hotel key card in the slot and fling the door open. Emerson and Mona are sitting on one of the beds sharing a pizza. Mona bolts from the room and hugs me tight.

"There is our girl detective." She sobs, obviously still overly emotional due to Emerson's return.

"It was my pleasure, Mona," I say, knowing that even though there is no monetary reward, it will look so awesome on my ever-growing amateur detective resume.

"You won third place. That's so awesome," Emerson shouts and joins in the hug. After a few seconds I peel them off of me. Detective Grant is standing back against the hall corridor looking grim.

"Can I talk to you alone for a minute, Aspen?" she asks, in a much more subdued tone. Rand gives me a warning look but I wink to let him know that I can handle her.

I walk into the hall and shut the door behind me. I jam my fists on my hips and fix a steely glance at Detective Grant. I feel sort of ridiculous standing here in an evening gown trying to look all badass, but I want her to take me seriously.

"How did you find Emerson?" she asks, almost timidly.

"Oh, the usual. Gathering clues, following up on leads, and my superior intuition on missing persons cases all played a big part." I'm not about to give her the satisfaction of knowing that I stumbled across Emerson and Cleve about to tie the knot while trying to stop Lucas and Angel's nuptials.

"Was she in danger?"

"Only if you consider marrying a billionaire octogenarian dangerous. Cleve Lynn had promised to bail out her family's debt if she married him. Emerson just so happens to be the doppelganger of the late Mrs. Lynn."

"Eww . . ." Detective Grant says, wrinkling her nose.

"It was beyond foul," I agree.

"You did a really good thing, Aspen. That detective was right about you."

I want to know what Harry said about me so bad that I can't hardly stand it but I'm not about to beg Detective Grant for anything.

"I could have used some help," I say, referring to her totally inadequate detecting skills.

"I know. I was wrong. I'm not trying to make excuses, but it's complicated," she says, pulling something out of a purse I didn't see on her arm.

"That's a genuine Coach bag," I say, stunned.

"Oh, yeah. I'm kind of a junkie," she admits.

"I prefer Dooneys but Coach would be my second choice."

She smiles and for a second it seems like we kind of bond. She hands me a plastic holder full of pictures. I look down to see the one she's turned it to. I recognize the photo immediately.

"You?" I ask in complete shock.

"Yes, I was Miss Teen Queen 1989. Andrea or Pageant Mistress, as you know her, was the first runner-up. She was convinced that I had slept with the judges to win. She made my life a living hell. She stalked me, and this was before they had stalking laws, so I couldn't do anything to stop her. Because of her I lost boyfriends, jobs, and basically had to go into hiding. She's the reason I went into law enforcement. When I could finally get a restraining order against her, it didn't matter. She had already ruined everything that meant anything to me. So I decided that I would make sure that didn't happen to anyone else."

"Wow. I mean, I knew she was nuts but I can't believe she kept that grudge against you this whole time just because she didn't win. That's creepy."

It was starting to make sense now why Detective

Grant didn't want to investigate. She would have had to immerse herself in the pageant world again and come face-to-face with someone who had terrorized her. And all this time she has been denying her outer beauty thinking it would help make a traumatic time in her life disappear. It always troubles me when people don't appreciate the effect designer makeup can have on their lives. But after my makeover, I don't think Detective Grant will be hiding her outer beauty anymore.

"It's not an excuse for failing your friend though. I let my personal feelings interfere with doing my job. I'm going to resign."

"That's crazy. That's like letting Pageant Mistress win. Don't let her control you anymore. Get your split ends trimmed, wear moisturizer, and please, get those eyebrows waxed," I beg her. She can't keep a straight face and starts cracking up.

"I haven't looked like this in a really long time," she says, admiring herself in a hallway mirror.

"You shouldn't let someone else control how you live your life or what you look like while you're living it."

"It's almost become a habit," she admits. "But it ends now. Pageant Mistress was already on probation for writing bad checks and petty theft. She sealed her fate when she attacked me today. The only pageant she'll be planning will be in the county jail. And thanks to you, Emerson is back with her mother and I feel better than I have in a long time."

She reaches forward in an awkward attempt to hug me. I close the gap and wrap my arms around her. She's not so bad after all.

"I think I'm going to go have a chat with Cleve Lynn," she says, pulling out of our hug.

"Can you charge him with anything?" I ask, crossing my fingers. I don't care if the man is old enough to be wearing adult diapers. What he did to Emerson, bribing her with indescribable amounts of money, was disgusting and I hope he gets locked up.

"Probably not. Since he didn't force her to marry him or take her against her will, I'll be hard-pressed to charge him with something, but believe me, I'm going to try."

"What if I told you that the Illusions hotel lets minors gamble and drink," I say, with a twinkle in my eye at remembering where Lucas had disappeared to after Angel broke up with him.

Detective Grant claps her unmanicured hands together excitedly. She flips open her cell phone and starts rattling off commands about setting up a sting at the Illusions hotel. She gives me a half-wave and then she is gone. Cleve Lynn is about to meet his match.

I open the hotel door to find Rand with a mouthful of pizza, flanked by Emerson and Mona.

"This one's a keeper," Mona says, squeezing Rand's forearm.

"Don't I know it," I agree, giving Rand a wink.

❂

"What you did for me was so great," Emerson says, kicking her Chuck Taylors against the curb in front of the hotel. She is on her way to the airport with Mona for their flight back to Illinois.

"Anybody would have done the same thing," I say modestly, knowing it's a total crock. It takes a very dedicated person to put their own life on hold to help someone else. What can I say, that's just who I am.

"I'm just glad you didn't end up marrying him," I say as shivers run down my spine. Money is awesome and I would love to have more of it, but I would never want it bad enough to sacrifice the rest of my life. "You and your mom are really smart women. You'll think of something to save the farm."

"Actually, we've already been brainstorming. We're thinking of a line of vintage tees. Look at this one," she says, grabbing a notebook out of her black carry-on. It's a sketch of a dancing cow. The caption says, "I like to mooove it, mooove it." I can't help but laugh even though it reminds me of Pageant Mistress making fun of my lasso moves.

"I think you've got a winner, Emerson. I'll take one in pink," I tell her. A taxi pulls up to the curb and loads their suitcases in the trunk.

"Have a safe trip home," I tell them, waving good-bye.

"I'm only going to ask you this one more time," Rand's voice says from behind me. "Are you ready to have some fun?"

"Oh yeah," I say, wrapping my arms around his neck and pulling him toward my lips.

@

Our last day in Vegas is perfect. Angel and I spend the morning dragging the boys through the Forum Shops to get some souvenirs. I could have scoured the Strip for treasures for hours but my feet had other ideas after practicing all week. So after a divine lunch at this fancy restaurant at the Wynn, we decide to head back to the hotel pool.

"Do I look okay in this?" I ask Angel, modeling my pageant bikini. She rolls her eyes and sticks her finger down her throat.

"You know you do, you conceited beyotch." She laughs.

I put my third-place sash on just for fun. Angel rolls her eyes as she ties on her bikini top.

"You are not going to wear that to the pool," she demands.

"I know. I'm just having fun. I'm proud of this. I worked hard for this sash."

"So the pageant circuit isn't what it's cracked up to be, huh?" She flops down on my bed to dry-shave her legs, which totally freaks me out.

"It's hard work. I mean, seriously, would you have ever thought I'd be happy coming in third?" We both crack up at the very thought of me ever being happy about being average.

"So are you really okay about you and Lucas not getting married?" I say, turning the conversation more serious.

"I was just testing him," she admits, not looking up from shaving her leg. "I've got to quit doing that."

"He loves you, Angel. Don't make him pay for your dad's mistakes." Lucas drives me crazy most of the time but I know, without a doubt, that he loves Angel. He cheated on me with her, for God's sake!

"I know. I'm trying."

"I'll help you. After all, that's what friends are for." I don't miss the brief misty-eyed glance Angel gives me. "Now hurry up. We don't want those pageant sluts hitting on our guys," I joke.

⊚

The afternoon is exactly how I pictured my spring break. Rand and I float along together in the water laughing about the entire week and how I always manage to get myself in such weird situations.

"I can't believe I actually saw you less this week than a normal week at school," Rand says.

"I'm sorry about that. I'm all done with mysteries though. I've got to start concentrating on my grades if I'm going to get into a good law school," I promise.

"Now I've heard it all." Rand laughs.

"What? Seriously. I'm turning in my girl detective cape. I'm not the least bit interested in disappearances or gossip anymore. All I'm interested in is living a life of leisure with my boy toy," I say, pretending like I'm pulling a cape from behind me and tossing it away.

Rand gives me a suspicious look. I slide on my sunglasses and recline my head back against the ledge of the pool.

"I heard someone saying something about a tiger missing from the exhibit at The Mirage," Rand says, trying to bait me.

"I don't do wildlife," I say, not looking up.

"There was a mention on the CNN ticker of Cleve Lynn marrying Lacy this morning."

"What?" I shout, losing my footing on the pool edge and nearly going underwater.

"I thought you didn't care about gossip and just wanted to live a life of leisure." He laughs.

"I can't believe she tricked him into marrying her," I say.

"Wouldn't you think it would be the other way around?" Rand asks, confused.

"Oh, no. She's wicked crafty, that one. She got him to marry her, knowing that he would probably be busted for something soon, and then she would have control of all his money." I shake my head in disbelief and a bit of admiration for the diabolical genius behind Lacy's plan.

"You could always try to stop her," Rand offers.

"Nah, let her have the money. It's all she's got," I say, relaxing back onto the pool ledge again.

"So are you saying that I actually have you all to myself? No more running off playing beauty queen, or putting yourself in dangerous situations?" Rand asks, swimming closer to me.

"I suppose that depends on your definition of dangerous," I say seductively, wrapping my legs around his waist and pulling him against me.

"How do you feel about loaded guns?" Rand laughs, pressing harder against me.

"Rand Bachrach, I can't believe you would talk to me like that," I say in fake outrage. "Do it again. It's hot." I laugh.

◎

I'm sitting in the hot tub watching Rand, Lucas, and Angel joke around together at the snack bar. For a few seconds it feels like time stops. I watch Angel toss her hair back and laugh. Lucas smacks Rand on the butt. Rand prances around with his butt pushed out, laughing.

Besides my parents, these three people are my world. I can't imagine where I would be without them. I wouldn't even want to. I slip out of the hot tub and wrap a towel around myself and walk over to join my best friends. With friends like these to have good times with I couldn't feel any luckier if I'd won a jackpot inside the casino. I've truly got it all.

☙

"Don't you dare," I warn Lucas, who has a tight grip on my arms and is threatening to throw me in the pool.

"DO IT! DO IT! DO IT!" Rand and Angel chant in unison.

"You jerks," I scream jokingly in midair right before I hit the lukewarm water that will totally ruin my hair and makeup.

I stay underwater for a few minutes, enjoying the muffled shouts of my friends above. I surface and swim over to the ladder. Rand holds out a tanned hand to help me out of the pool. He looks so handsome in his navy blue swim trunks. His curls are still damp from an earlier swim and his muscular chest is beaded with water droplets. I can't stop staring at him.

He pulls me out and leads me over to a deck chair that he covered with an extra-large beach towel. I stretch out on it, keeping my eyes on him the whole time.

"What's wrong?" he asks, looking self-conscious.

"I just don't understand it," I say, squeezing the excess water from my hair.

"What?" he asks, confused.

"How I can love you more than anything else in the world."

"Even more than Dooneys?" he asks, wide-eyed.

"Way more than Dooneys." I laugh, intertwining my fingers with his in a motion so perfect and automatic that I don't even have to think about it.

Things to Do on Spring Break When You're Broke

BY ASPEN BROOKS

1) Have a rummage sale and save all the proceeds to go toward next year's spring break.
2) Hang out with your parents and totally suck up so they'll spot you some cash to go away next year.
3) Volunteer in your community.
4) Get a seasonal job.
5) Get a head start on studying for finals.
6) Read more books by Stephanie Hale.
7) Spend some time with your siblings. No matter what they say, they really miss having you at home.
8) Throw a spring break luau and invite all your friends who didn't go away.
9) Go to the library and check out a book on spa treatments. Then spend a couple of days just pampering yourself.
10) Scour the Internet to find the best place to go next year!